He was…

…going to kis[ ] second before [ ] mouth found hers. The very one she'd been dreaming about, fantasising over.

He tasted like dill-pickle chips, ginger ale and something dark and thrillingly wicked. *Like sin*, she realised as her body melted against his. Her knees grew weak and her legs wobbled, forcing her even closer to him. Heat moved through her limbs and settled hotly in her sex, triggering a deep throb in her womb. She sighed, savouring the feel of him against her body. Her soft to his hard, strong hands framing her face, sliding into her hair and kneading her scalp.

Heaven.

Dear Reader,

Welcome back to my MEN OUT OF UNIFORM series! I've had such a wonderful response from my readers for these hard-living and loving heroes. They're hot. They're strong. They're Southern gentlemen. They're former Rangers, bona fide badasses and all-around true heroes. Furthermore, there's nothing better than a man in uniform…unless it's a man out of one.

Ranger Lucas "Huck" Finn has spent the past twelve years in the military as part of an elite paratrooper unit. But when an accident during a training mission blows his knee, Huck finds himself looking for a new career. When Colonel Carl Garrett suggests that he meet with the guys at Ranger Security, Huck instantly leaps at the chance. And leaps right into the mission of a lifetime.

His first assignment for Ranger Security involves guarding Atlanta socialite Sapphira Stravos. Going from a decorated paratrooper to almost-crippled babysitter for a seemingly spoiled doggy-toting debutante is almost more than he can bear. He soon learns, however, that there's more to Sapphira than meets the eye. And what's meeting the eye is damned hard to resist.

I love to hear from my readers, so please visit my website – www.readRhondaNelson.com – or visit me at my group blog, www.soapboxqueens.com, with fellow authors and friends Jennifer LaBrecque and Vicki Lewis Thompson. We're always hosting some sort of party in our magical castle.

Happy reading,

Rhonda Nelson

THE BODYGUARD

BY
RHONDA NELSON

First published in Great Britain 2009
Harlequin Mills & Boon Limited,
Eton House, 18-24 Paradise Road, Richmond, Surrey TW9 1SR

© Rhonda Nelson 2008
(Original title *The Loner*)

ISBN: 978 0 263 87488 4

14-0809

Harlequin Mills & Boon policy is to use papers that are natural, renewable
and recyclable products and made from wood grown in sustainable
forests. The logging and manufacturing processes conform to the legal
environmental regulations of the country of origin.

Printed and bound in Spain
by Litografia Rosés S.A., Barcelona

Rhonda Nelson, a Waldenbooks bestselling author, two-time RITA® Award nominee and *Romantic Times BOOKreviews* Reviewers' Choice nominee, writes hot romantic comedy for the Blaze® line. In addition to a writing career she has a husband, two adorable kids, a black Lab and a beautiful bichon frisé who dogs her every step. She and her family make their chaotic but happy home in a small town in northern Alabama.

This book is dedicated to Misty Pierce,
my "first" reader. Thanks so much, Mis,
for always being such a cheerleader
for my writing, even in its earliest form.
I'm so glad that you're a part of our family.

Prologue

"OH, SHIT," Lucas "Huck" Finn muttered, using every trick he'd learned as a U.S. Army Ranger—particularly those in Jump school—to guide his parachute toward the drop zone he instinctively knew he was going to miss. Call it a sixth sense, a premonition, a damn psychic moment, hell he didn't give a damn.

He just knew he was screwed.

And on a friggin' training mission at that, one where *he* was running point. Because he'd been thinking about his father again, a man he'd never even met. Why? Who knew? Curiosity? Closure? He didn't have any idea, but he couldn't deny the faceless parent had been on his mind a lot in recent months. He'd even begun making inquiries, trying to find out the identity of the man. No luck yet, but the P.I. he'd hired assured him that it was only a matter of time.

Cheeks burning, he hit the call button on the radio. "I'm north of the DZ," he said tightly.

"North, sir?"

Bloody hell. "I've overshot the drop zone," he clarified, mortification making his voice gruff. Two-hundred-plus drops, HALO training—High Altitude, Low Opening—almost a decade of experience and, while he'd had some pretty scary things happen while stealthily floating through the skies for Uncle Sam, this was the first time in *years* he'd scuttled a training exercise. He'd once landed in an eight-by-eight square of beach at high tide between two rocky outcroppings amid enemy fire and *still* stuck the landing, for Pete's sake. He swore again and struggled with the lines to pull himself back on target.

In vain, he knew. Still…

"You're going to be in the trees, Major," Dennis Jenkins told him, as if he didn't know. Even if it wasn't nearing midnight and even if he didn't know every inch of Fort Benning, Georgia, like the back of his hand, it was hard to miss the looming shadows of the treetops reaching up from the ground like ragged fingers trying to catch him.

The last damn thing any paratrooper wanted to do was land in a tree—too many chances for injury—but in this case, given the rocky terrain, steep hills and valleys on this particular stretch of ground, something told him he'd be better off kissing an oak tree than landing on uncertain terra firma.

"I'm coming in," Huck told him as the earth loomed ever closer.

"You want me to send a crew?"

"Hell, yeah. I don't want to walk out of here, dammit." He could cut himself free and get out of the tree, but hoofing it several miles back to the heart of the base in the dark was unnecessary. Doable, of course, but unnecessary.

"Roger that," Jenkins said.

Huck tripped the switch on his flashlight, illuminating the bit of air right above his feet, trying to gauge the best place to come in.

Unfortunately there wasn't one.

Trees, trees and more trees.

He swore again, worked the lines to slow his descent and drew his legs up in an attempt to keep them out of harm's way. He felt the first branch scrape his thigh, a second scratch his face as he plunged into skinny pine tree. Soft wood, weak branches, he thought dimly as his parachute finally snagged and took hold, momentarily jerking him upward again, pushing the breath from his lungs.

Before he could take stock of the situation, he heard an ominous crack and was free-falling once more. His flashlight swung in an illuminated beam through the forest as he plunged downward. He felt his right arm break as he tumbled from branch to branch, a stinging sensation in his side—no doubt a puncture wound— then a horrible mind-blowing, gut-wrenching pain so intense it made his mind go white then black and then back to gray, and then another ominous crack as his knee struck another limb and bent at an unnatural angle.

Huck suddenly stopped falling, hovered upside down roughly ten feet from the ground. He could hear the hum of the jeep engine powering on in the distance. Under ordinary circumstances he would have pulled his knife and sliced the lines, but considering the extent of his injuries he knew better.

So much for walking out of here, he thought with bitter irony, struggling to stay conscious. His world faded in and out of focus and his strained, breathless curses turned the air blue around him. Given the stupid mistake he'd just made, he knew he would be lucky to ever walk again.

Years wasted, he thought, fighting the pain, panic and blackness threatening to consume him.

Career over.

And with that thought…nothing.

1

Three months later...

"ARE ABSOLUTELY certain this is what you want to do?" Colonel Carl Garrett asked, his tone as grave as his expression.

Seated in an uncomfortable chair in front of the colonel's desk, Huck nodded. "Yes, sir."

"You could still be an asset to the military, Major Finn. Just because you're no longer physically able to meet the demands of an active Ranger doesn't mean that you are no longer of value to your country. You have other talents as well," he said, carefully perusing the documents on his gleaming mahogany desk. "You could be very useful in an instructional capacity if you—"

Huck bit back a blistering curse. "With all due respect, sir, I didn't join the military to *teach*. I joined to *defend*."

And he couldn't do that anymore. Would never be able to do that again.

He swallowed, pushed back the despair, anger and absolute fury roiling in his gut. How could he have been so stupid? Have made such a rookie mistake? His knee twinged, remembering, and his fist involuntarily tightened around his cane. "I know that there are lots of other men who've made the transition that you're talking about, Colonel, and I respect their decision. However, it's not the path for me. I'm a man of action, sir, and since I'm no longer capable of *acting*, I know that leaving the military is the best route."

For him, it was the *only* route.

Because Huck had never considered a life outside of serving Uncle Sam, he'd never recognized the need to draw up a contingency plan. Lots of fellow soldiers had made inquiries as to his plans once he'd decided to leave, but he could hardly tell them when he didn't know himself. All he knew at this point was that he *had* to get out. That being here, being wounded, being unable to perform his job, was slowly eating away at the few tangled shreds of sanity he had left.

No matter what Garrett said, he was useless now. Dead weight. A liability to his unit.

And just like when a lady always knew when to leave—the kind he made it a point to date—a has-been Ranger knew to heed the exit cue as well.

Where would he go? Hell, who knew? At this point he didn't even care. He just wanted to get away from here. Thankfully he had enough money in the bank to coast for a while until he could figure out the next chapter in his life. He could always go home, he knew. Home being Red Rock, Georgia, a little town that sat right outside Savannah. Close enough for his mother to drive in every day to clean and cater to the city's upper crust, but far enough away to always remember his place, Huck thought bitterly.

And God knows he never forgot.

Between the snotty rich kids he sometimes crossed paths with while his mother was working and the efficient grapevine of a small town, Huck had never had a problem forgetting he was a bastard child born to a young unwed mother, one he grimly suspected had been taken advantage of by one of the smug, entitled bastards she'd cleaned up after. Had his mother ever told him this? No. But he'd caught enough snippets of conversation between his mother and grandmother while he'd been growing up to rouse his suspicions.

Following her lead, Huck had never asked about his father. He'd been loved enough without a father—it had seemed to be her personal goal, a guilt she'd carried and couldn't shake—and he'd instinctively known that asking about someone who clearly hadn't given a damn about either of them would cause her undue grief.

And that, of course, had been unacceptable.

His mother would welcome him back with open arms, but somehow burdening her with his new problems—when he'd joined the military to free her of them to start with—seemed particularly counterproductive.

After years of cleaning up after the idle rich, Beth Finn had finally saved enough money to start her own business and no one was prouder of her than Huck. A firm believer in the power of sugar—of the perfect cookie, specifically—his mother had opened a cookie bakery. Snickerdoodles specialized in its namesake, of course, as well as beautiful iced cookies that were packaged as cookie bouquets. Her online business, in particular, had taken off. He inwardly smiled. He received a care package from her every Friday like clockwork.

Keeping her in the dark after his injury had been particularly hard, but Huck simply hadn't been able to tell her and had forbid anyone else from sharing the information with her as well. She would have put everything on hold—including the brand-new business that needed her—in order to come to Fort Benning and take care of him. He'd let her help take care of him until he'd turned eighteen, then he'd earned an ROTC scholarship, joined the program at the University of Alabama—Roll Tide!—and the rest, as they say, was history.

At fourteen he'd watched her tiredly sit at the kitchen table—the familiar scent of bleach and starch clinging to her small hands and curly hair—and wryly debate the merit of buying him new shoes to replace the ones he'd outgrown within a month or pay the phone bill. "The phone's a nuisance, anyway," she'd said, ruffling his hair while he'd burned with shame, mad at his feet for having the audacity to grow and put another burden on her slim shoulders. To be so small, she'd always been a remarkably strong woman.

The next day after school he'd gone down to the local co-op and hung around, pestering the farmers until he had enough work lined up to cover the phone bill and then some. Initially she'd protested, had told him to save his money, that she'd take care of them, but Huck had insisted. He was young and strong, perfectly capable of mucking stalls and hauling hay, all of which he'd done. There'd been a sense of pride along with the accomplishment, a measure of satisfaction in knowing that he could contribute.

And he still contributed, unbeknownst to her.

Despite the fact that he no longer lived at home, he'd set up a retirement account for his mother and had been making monthly deposits for the past ten years.

As for the mystery surrounding his father, he found it highly ironic that his preoccupation with the man had ultimately cost him his career. It was funny, Huck thought now. He'd never really given the man a second thought until a fellow trooper had lost his father and then Huck had suddenly been consumed with curiosity. What sort of man got a girl pregnant and just walked away? Had he married? Had children? Had he ever spared a thought for him and his mother?

No matter how much he tried to tell himself none of it mattered…he couldn't quite put it to rest. He hated himself for it, but couldn't deny it all the same. That's why he'd ultimately hired an investigator. He had to know. And now, thanks to his accident, he'd get to find out who the bastard was and hopefully administer a belated payback. He warmed with purpose, felt the first stirrings of adrenaline hit his bloodstream. God, how he'd missed it. Could it rival jumping headfirst out of a plane at twenty thousand feet? No. But it would do.

It had to.

Garrett stared at him for a full five seconds longer,

waiting for more of an explanation, Huck supposed. But one he wouldn't get. "You're set on this?"

"I am."

"And I can't change your mind?"

Huck looked him dead in the eye. "No, sir."

"In that case—" he scrawled his signature across Huck's release papers "—might I make a suggestion?"

An old warhorse with a voice seasoned with piss and gravel, Colonel Carl Garrett was a legendary figure at Fort Benning. Despite having more than thirty years under his belt, he clearly had no plan to retire at any point in the near future. Huck envied him so much in that moment it hurt. Garrett had purpose, knew his place, had been able to adapt from strapping young soldier to mature commander seemingly with ease.

Furthermore and most importantly, if the man wanted to make a suggestion regarding his future, Huck would be a fool not to listen.

"Certainly, sir."

"I knew the moment I'd heard of your unfortunate injury that we'd lost you, Major Finn. As you so aptly put it, you're a man of action." Garrett smiled. "Men of action don't typically do well chained to a desk or tethered to a classroom." His gaze drifted over the cane across Huck's knees. "It's our loss, of course, because despite knowing what I know, I still think our up-and-comers could benefit from your expertise."

Be that as it may, Huck thought, he wasn't changing his mind.

"Nonetheless, when I heard that you'd been injured,

I knew you were on your way out. As such, I took the liberty of forwarding your information to some friends of mine. They're former Rangers like yourself, based in Atlanta—Ranger Security," he said, quirking a bushy brow. "You might have heard of it."

Every sense went on point. As a matter of fact, he had heard of it. Jamie Flanagan, Brian Payne and Guy McCann were legendary at Fort Benning, and their success in the security business post military was equally famous amid his counterparts on base. Come to think of it, he'd actually gone through a special ops training class with Brian Payne and Danny Levinson, a fallen comrade who paid the ultimate price for Uncle Sam. Levinson had been a good friend of all three men and their exit out of the military was rumored to be somehow related to Danny's death.

Though he'd never actually considered contacting them, something about the idea of working with them— with men from his world—made his gut clench with hope and his spine prickle with anticipation.

He cast a glance at his ruined knee and mentally watched the idea disintegrate. Hell, who was he kidding? Sure, he could walk—had forced himself to run as well though it hurt like a son of a bitch—but even a security specialist would have to pass certain physical assessment tests and he knew damn well he'd never make the cut.

"They're aware of your injuries, Finn," Garrett said, using that uncanny ability to read his mind. "They're still interested. You have a job waiting for you should you wish to accept it."

Huck blinked, stunned. "Waiting for me? Without an interview? Without assessing my physical ability to do the job?"

Garrett merely smiled. "Your record combined with my recommendation is more than enough."

"But what about my knee? I can't—"

"The only thing you *can't* do, Major Finn, is jump out of airplanes anymore. You are more than physically capable of joining Ranger Security and taking on the cases you'll be assigned."

Ah… So that was the lay of it. His gaze hardened. "I won't be anyone's pity project, Colonel, regardless of—"

"Only a fool would pity you, Major," Garrett interrupted. "I merely hate to see your talent and training squandered. I thought it would be a good fit, sent your file along with my own comments regarding your character, which has not been injured." He shrugged. "The rest is up to you. Take it or don't, the choice is yours. It's a plan, at any rate, and I'm guessing that when you came in here today, short of getting me to sign your release papers, you didn't have one."

At that, Huck had to grin. Garrett more than likely had more enemies than friends, but the old bastard sure as hell knew how to read a man. What else could he see? Huck wondered, shooting him an uneasy look.

"Nothing firm, sir," he finally admitted.

"Give it some thought then," Garrett told him. "What have you got to lose?"

At this point…nothing, Huck realized, releasing a

pent-up breath. His career was blown right along with his knee. In fact, right now the only thing he was at risk of losing was his mind.

"YOU CAN'T BE SERIOUS," Sapphira Stravos breathed, staring at her father. Trixie, her Maltese and perpetual companion, shivered in her lap, evidently feeling the chill in the air despite the balmy ninety-degree heat they were enjoying out by her father's pool in Atlanta's elite Buckhead area.

"I'm dead serious. I've received two threats on your life. To ignore another would imply that I am foolish or don't care about your welfare, neither of which is accurate."

Not if you asked her, Sapphira thought with a mental eyeroll. Did Mathias Stravos care for her? Sure. He cared for her in the same way he cared for his prized Thoroughbred horses, his vintage Bentley, the prime piece of real estate they currently sat on.

She was a *possession,* not a daughter.

Sapphira swallowed and ran her hand over Trixie's slim back. She hadn't been a daughter since the moment her older brother, Nicholas, had committed suicide four years ago. Rather than risk the emotional upheaval of losing another child, her father had recompartmentalized her role.

He'd moved her out of the column of "family" and inserted her into "belongings."

No doubt the same fate would have awaited her mother, but she'd left the minute the funeral was over and Saphhira rarely heard from her. "Sapphira's as good as dead, too," she'd heard her mother tell him. "You'll kill her the same way you murdered my Nicky."

Not true, Sapphira knew, but she wasn't so certain her father did. Had her father pushed Nicky? Expected a lot out of him as the heir apparent to the Stravos fortune? Certainly. But that hadn't been what had driven her troubled brother over the edge. Though Sapphira had her suspicions, Nicky had taken that secret to the grave with him.

And, God, how she missed him…

Funny how life could change in the blink of an eye. She'd been one week away from graduation, had already accepted a position—one that she knew she'd earned though she knew there would have been rumblings to the contrary at Stravos Industries—when Nicky had taken enough tranquilizers to drop an elephant. In one fell swoop she'd lost her brother, mother and father—her entire family—and any future she had of making a genuine career for herself.

Convinced that he'd driven Nicky over the edge, her father had promptly killed the job—despite her railing and her tears—then had made it clear that he would professionally annihilate anyone who hired her—and he had the clout to do it. He'd immediately put her on salary, though she had no title and no particular job. The only thing that had saved her was her charity work, and she'd had to keep that as low profile as possible or risk his wrath.

Fearing she would crack as well, he didn't want her to do *anything*.

"You're an heiress, dammit. Go shopping. Go to the

spa. Tour Europe. But you're not *going to work. I've worked hard so that you don't have to. Not taking advantage of the wealth that you've been given is a direct insult to me—and I will not be insulted."*

At any rate, Sapphira knew her father cared for her out of obligation now and not out of love. It would be easier to resent him if she didn't understand, but unfortunately she did. Nicky's death had paralyzed her father with grief, had emotionally bankrupted him. Every once in a while she'd catch him staring at her brother's picture—the one he kept on his desk—and the haunted look of pain on his face was enough to bring tears to her eyes. In his own misguided way, she knew he was trying to protect her—didn't want to push her the way he had Nicky. He treated her as though she were one of his prizewinning rare orchids—lovely to look at, delicate and frail.

Regardless, hiring a bodyguard for her due to a couple of newspaper-clipping-and-paste threats was ridiculous.

"Daddy, don't you think you're going a bit overboard? Why would anyone possibly want to hurt me?"

Her father gestured to Rosa, his personal servant who dogged his every step, for another drink. "You don't achieve my level of success without making a few enemies, Sapphira." He shot her a dark look. "Furthermore, I've heard rumblings about your recent activities—"

A dart of panic landed in her chest. He couldn't have— She'd been so careful—

"—and Cindy Ward's father, in particular, is displeased."

Sapphira felt a tremulous smile of relief slide over her numb lips. So he didn't know about her work. Thank God. "Cindy's a vital asset to Belle Charities," she told him. "She's got a wonderful way of making people open their wallets for a good cause."

He snorted. "That way is called *blackmail,* Sapphira. She threatened to out her own brother, for pity's sake."

Too true, she knew, feeling a grin slide across her lips. Cindy Ward was the perfect Atlanta socialite. A proud member of the country club, she shopped at all the right stores, attended all the right parties and kept up with every bit of dirt.

On everybody.

She was stubborn, opinionated, big-hearted and generous. She was also one of the best friends Sapphira had ever had.

"You're not going to change my mind about this, Sapphira. I've already contacted an agency and have arranged for your care. A security specialist will be arriving first thing tomorrow morning."

She gulped. "Tomorrow morning?"

"That's right. I've contracted Ranger Security. They'll be looking into the matter, tracing the source of the letters, and will provide twenty-four-hour security."

Twenty-four-hour security? Surely he didn't mean— "What do you mean twenty-four-hour security?" she asked, a big ball of dread bouncing in her gut. They'd have to file reports with her father, chronicle her comings and goings. She swallowed the nausea creeping up her throat.

"Exactly what I said," he told her, frowning. "Round-the-clock care."

"A round-the-clock babysitter? Because of two little letters?" she said, her voice escalating with outrage. She reached for her hand sanitizer—aka her fix—and vigorously rubbed it into her palms.

"You're the intended target of those two little letters."

She had to admit when she'd seen them she'd gotten a bit of a chill. *Your daughter's in danger. Sapphira's not safe.* Still… A twenty-four-hour bodyguard?

"For how long?"

"As long as it takes, Sapphira. I've researched the local security companies. Ranger Security is at the top of their field. Every agent is a former Ranger. They're smart, competent and trained in lethal force. You're completely safe in their hands."

She wasn't worried so much about being safe as she was about being watched. If her father had gone to the trouble to hire a bodyguard, no doubt that bodyguard would be making regular reports to her dad.

Not good.

She'd worked hard to cover her tracks, to make sure that her father hadn't found out just how far she'd taken Belle Charities. He was under the impression that she and a few friends got together over manies and pedies and doled out a small portion of their allowances. If he had any idea that she'd turned it into a multimillion-dollar charitable organization—complete with an underground staff she managed—as well as her regular trips into the inner city to mentor unwed mothers, he'd not only freak, he'd cut her off.

The realization made her stomach lurch.

She had too many people depending on her to let that happen. Programs in place that provided scholarships, food, medical care—the things she *personally* financed with her so-called salary. She couldn't let them down.

Wouldn't.

Furthermore, what about Carmen? She was due any day now and Sapphira had promised to be in the delivery room with her. How was she supposed to attend OB visits and birthing classes with a freaking bodyguard in tow? She rubbed more sanitizer into her palms. Good grief, what a nightmare.

Though she'd tried to stay focused on providing help and keeping an emotional distance, something about Carmen Martinez had inexplicably tugged at Sapphira's heartstrings. Petite yet fierce, Carmen was smart and hardworking, resourceful and funny. At seventeen she was awfully young to be a mother, but despite her circumstances looked forward to it all the same. There was a maturity in her that wasn't often seen in one so young, a wry but resigned wit at her dire circumstances. No family—her foster parents had kicked her out when they'd discovered the pregnancy—no support and no boyfriend. Evidently the college boy—one whose family Sapphira knew rather well—who'd positively adored her before her pregnancy suddenly remembered he had a girlfriend and couldn't be burdened by a baby.

Too bad, Sapphira thought, eyes narrowing. There was nothing to be done at the moment, but the instant the baby was born, she planned to make sure the father was named in a paternity suit. In fact, she planned to personally cover the attorney's fees.

When she'd first decided to mentor, Sapphira knew it had been her way of coping with her own unplanned teenage pregnancy. Though it seemed like a lifetime ago and though she'd lost her baby early on, she'd never completely gotten over the paralyzing fear of being pregnant at such an early age and losing her baby…

Losing her baby, despite the wrath and ridicule she would have faced from her parents, had broken something inside of her. She'd been seventeen, in love in only the way a teenager could be—wide-eyed, wholeheartedly, head over heels to the point of destruction. A whispered promise, a bottle of wine and an "I love you" later, she'd parted with her virginity without protection and a month later both her period and the boyfriend were MIA. She'd been so panicked, so ashamed, but so hopeful over her baby. She might have been young, but she'd loved her baby from the minute she'd seen the positive sign on her home-pregnancy test.

Even hopeful and afraid, she'd felt alienated from everyone. Telling her parents would have been a nightmare and facing Ella, her beloved nanny, heartbreaking. Nicky? Out of the question. Unfortunately, she'd lost the baby—it had been Ella who'd found her, weeping and bleeding on the bathroom floor…and her life had never been the same.

Mentoring had been her way to help, to manifest the change she'd gone through as a result of that experience, and Carmen... Well, Carmen reminded her a lot of herself.

"I don't have a problem with the security, Dad," she finally said, careful to keep the panic out of her voice because he was so shrewd he'd surely recognize it. "But I don't want a stranger spending the night in my home."

"You're welcome to move back into the main house— where I can protect you—until the threat is neutralized," he offered, knowing full well it was out of the question.

The sprawling Greek Revival mansion her father had built in honor of their heritage had always been too big and impersonal to her. In fact, from the time she'd been a little girl she'd hated it. Even her room had felt too large and many a night she'd dragged a pillow and blanket into her walk-in closet and spent the night on the floor. They'd always made a joke of it, but Sapphira preferred intimate spaces.

Frankly, she'd preferred her nanny's quarters and had spent more time at Ella's than at home. She'd loved it so much her father had built a replica of Ella's small cottage for her next door to her beloved friend after Nicky had died. The older Cajun-French woman had always been more like a grandmother to her than hired help and Sapphira knew Ella loved her regardless of her paycheck. True, Ella had been reimbursed for caring for her day-to-day needs when she was growing up, but Sapphira knew she'd genuinely *cared* for her all the same. She'd always been able to draw comfort from that, to know that she was loved unconditionally.

When she'd gotten too old for a nanny and had heard her parents discussing the need to let Ella go, Sapphira had become inconsolable. She'd always had a strong bond with her nanny, one that she knew her mother had resented. Clarise Stravos had kept insisting that Ella had to go, but thankfully her father had taken pity on her and kept Ella on in a household-management capacity.

Her mother had never been particularly…motherly. She wasn't affectionate, didn't want her clothes being mussed with hugs. She'd always kept her children at a polite distance, preferring to take them out to show them off during dinner parties, then eagerly shooing them away the moment the oohing and aahing had subsided. She might have been her biological mother, but she'd never been truly there for her.

She'd never been a momma.

No, Ella had been and was her rock, had nursed her through the chicken pox, scraped knees, first heartbreak, second heartbreak and even third heartbreak, Sapphira thought wryly, not to mention the miscarriage. She'd been a soft shoulder to cry on when she'd lost Nicky and the rest of her family. "Come here, *ma chère,*" she'd said. "Everythin's gonna be all right."

And she was the only person who knew exactly what she did with her time and money. And why.

"Ella's right next door," Sapphira pointed out, knowing it was a weak argument.

Her father snorted. "Ella's an old woman. She can't protect you."

"We live in a freaking fortress," she told him, exasperated. A ten-foot stone fence surrounded their estate, as well as a gate at the only entrance to the property. Her father had a top-notch, high-tech-security system complete with motion detectors and closed-circuit cameras. "Short of a person parachuting onto the grounds, I'm safe here, Dad."

"You'll be safer with a bodyguard. End of discussion, Sapphira," he said, picking up his newspaper. And just like that, she might as well have vanished. She felt her jaw ache and narrowly avoided grinding her teeth.

Furthermore, it might be the end of the discussion, Sapphira thought, bristling at his oh-so-*gallingly*-familiar autocratic tone. But it sure as hell wasn't the end of the battle. She might not be able to change her father's mind, but she could certainly play the spoiled debutante to the point that her bodyguard would *want* to quit. If there was one thing she'd learned as a Stravos captive it was how to outmaneuver a master.

Bring on the former Ranger, she thought, warming to her plan as she fed Trixie a bite of kibble.

She'd be his worst freakin' nightmare.

2

"I'M TELLING YOU, I'm going to kick somebody's ass if one of you bastards doesn't relieve me soon."

The two men seated around the phone from which the angry voice originated merely smiled. "We've done our time. Man up, McCann. Didn't you say she was 'just a girl'? 'A pampered debutante'?"

Though he knew he should clear his throat to alert Brian Payne and Jamie Flanagan of his presence, Huck found himself too intrigued instead and decided to eavesdrop just a moment longer. Their secretary—a man who'd introduced himself as Juan-Carlos, and who, interestingly, hadn't been the least surprised to see him—had told him where to find the owners of Ranger Security, after all. Evidently Juan-Carlos had been with them since the company's inception, a fact the he was exceedingly proud of. He'd given Huck a sort of knowing smile, one that plainly let him know that he didn't have a real clue as to what he was getting into.

"I don't give a damn what I said," McCann said tightly, his voice muffled a bit as if he was cupping the phone, angling for some privacy from the sounds of it.

"If I have to fetch one more freakin' latte *for the dog,* I'm going to lose it. I'm a security specialist, not a damn pooch-sitting service."

Unable to help himself, Huck chuckled, drawing their attention from the comfy armchairs they currently occupied in the sleek downtown Atlanta high-rise.

Payne and Flanagan looked at him, then back to each other and shared a significant smile. "Hang tight, McCann. Your relief just walked through the door."

"My relief? But—"

Flanagan leaned forward and disconnected the call, then stood and made his way over to Huck. He smiled, somewhat gratefully. "You must be Lucas Finn," he said, offering his hand. "We've been waiting for you."

Waiting for him? Now, that was interesting, he thought, his gaze sliding between the two men. "You can call me Huck."

Cool and subtly intimidating, Payne joined them as well. "It's good to see you again, Major Finn." So he remembered him, Huck thought, a bit surprised. But he shouldn't have been. If memory served, Payne's nickname had been the Specialist. Clearly the man didn't miss a damn thing. Payne gestured back to the seating area. "Can I get you something to drink?"

"No, thanks," Huck said, lowering himself into a chair. Unwilling to show a bit of weakness, he'd left his cane at his hotel room for this meeting. He'd actually been in town a few days—and had been home before that, visiting his mother and grandmother, cautiously poking around for information on his father to pass along to his P.I.—but wanted to do a little bit more research on Ranger Security on his own before he formally accepted the job. Knowing that the men were former Rangers and had come with Garrett's seal of approval was enough, of course, but Huck didn't like walking into any situation blind.

Furthermore, what he'd discovered had impressed the hell out of him and, considering he was damaged goods, he found himself eternally thankful that a company of their standards would want him at all. Unless the information on their Web site wasn't current—a fact he completely doubted—he would be their first hire outside of the core group.

And judging from the call he'd just overheard, they were in dire need of new blood.

"We're assuming since you're here, you're interested in taking the job," Flanagan said.

"I am," Huck said, nodding.

"I'm sure you have some questions," Payne remarked, handing Flanagan a high-energy drink, before taking his own seat. He shot him a look and waited expectantly.

Huck felt an awkward smile slide over his lips and he passed a hand over his face, attempting to wipe it off. Actually, there was one burning question he'd like answered. "Why me?" he asked. "No doubt you could have your pick of much better qualified applicants. Hell, I didn't even *apply,* but was merely referred."

Flanagan and Payne shared another one of those unspoken looks. Huck didn't speak the language, but had shared the same sort of bond with members of his team. Men that were still getting to do the job he wasn't, he thought, beating back the envy that tangled around his heart. At present he had to admit he'd treated the majority of his friends like shit. After the accident, he'd been so ashamed—of both the mistake and his envy— he'd basically cut off contact.

Mick Chivers and Levi McPherson, both of whom he'd known since college, were the only friends who'd been able to withstand his brutal sarcasm and ultimate freeze-out, and they'd been the only friends who'd understood why he couldn't stay in the military. When Huck had first mentioned the Ranger Security idea to Mick, his daredevil look-death-in-the-eye-and-spit friend had been a little in awe, which had somehow made joining the company feel less like a cop-out and more like a real plan. Levi—who epitomized the strong, silent type—had only offered one word. "Cool." Huck had promised to report in and let them know how things were going as soon as he was settled.

"Let me ask you a question," Flanagan said. "Before you walked in here this morning, did you research our company? Check us out through the Better Business Bureau? Contact some of our former clients? Did you run any sort of background check on one or more of us? Did you use your contacts in the military to research our service records?"

Though it would probably piss them off that he'd checked up on them, Huck had no intention of lying. "Of course," he admitted. "I did my homework. Frankly, I wanted to know what sort of men would hire a guy sight unseen without so much as the benefit of an interview."

Flanagan's face split in a wide grin. "Exactly. And that's what we're looking for." He took another pull from his energy drink. "Here's the thing, Finn. I split time between here and Maine, a fact I'm sure you ran across during your inquiry," he added, quirking a brow.

Huck nodded. Surprisingly, Flanagan was married to Garrett's granddaughter, Audrey, who ran a destressing camp for burned-out execs and harried mothers.

"I've got a toddler and another baby on the way." He gestured to Payne. "Payne and McCann are both new fathers. While we love the business, our priorities have shifted a bit. We all want more time with our families. Thankfully, our business has grown to the point that we're in a position to add to our staff, but we're not willing to compromise on quality. We believe former Rangers make the best security specialists. Furthermore, as I'm sure you're aware, there is a certain regard and camaraderie among those with shared experiences."

A grin rolled around Payne's lips. "In other words, if it ain't broke, don't fix it."

Huck chuckled, feeling more relaxed by the minute.

"Given our special requirements, when we decided to hire another agent the first person we contacted was Colonel Garrett," Payne said. "He's in an excellent position at Fort Benning to alert us to possible recruits. He knows us, knows our standards and knows the kind of man we're looking for. We called him seven months ago, Finn, and you're the *only* person he's referred." He paused, allowing the statement to penetrate. "You weren't *merely referred*—you were chosen."

Chosen. Huck swallowed, honored more than he could have ever imagined.

"We're aware of your injuries, Finn," Flanagan told him. "But we know enough about your character to know that they aren't going to limit you beyond what you need to do here."

Payne released a pent-up breath. "And right now what we need you to do is handle security duty for a certain Atlanta socialite who is, frankly, driving us all crazy."

Huck grinned. So that's what they'd meant when they'd told McCann his relief had just gotten there.

"We've all taken turns with her, and McCann is—as I'm sure you heard—about to come unglued," Flanagan told him, chuckling softly. He pushed a hand through his hair. "I swear I think she's doing it on purpose."

Payne grimaced. "I don't give a damn why she's doing it. I just want to be through with her. Has Guy had any luck tracing the letters?" he asked Jamie.

Flanagan shook his head, then explained for Huck's benefit. "Evidently her father is concerned that she's in danger. So far we haven't had any luck isolating the threat."

Huck frowned. "Letters, you say?"

"Postmarked Atlanta, so they're local. Cut—with pinking shears, not traditional scissors—from the newspaper. And they're clean. No fingerprints."

Intriguing. "Why would anyone want to hurt her?"

"Well, Guy wants to hurt her because she keeps making him run pointless errands for her dog," Payne said, smiling. "Aside from that, all we have to go on is what her father says."

"And what does he say?" Huck asked.

"Mathias Stravos says he's been in business long enough to make substantial enemies. We've done a little poking around and that's certainly true. He's a real estate mogul who has greased more than a few palms when it comes to zoning issues and the like. Still," Flanagan hedged, shaking his head, "something about it doesn't feel right. The letters merely say that Sapphira's not safe, that she's in danger. They aren't threatening, per se, but I could see where her father couldn't ignore them."

"Sapphira?" Now, *that* was an interesting name.

"They're Greek," Payne explained. He picked up a folder and handed it to Huck. "Here's an employment agreement," he said. "Terms, policies and whatnot. Flanagan, McCann and I all have apartments in the building. We like being close and will expect our future agents to be as well. As such, I have recently purchased the building next door and while the renovations aren't complete, there's a ground-floor apartment that is ready for immediate occupancy. It's yours and is part of your employment package."

Flanagan, who'd exited the room, returned carrying a laptop case, cell phone, handgun and permit to carry concealed. "These are yours as well," he said. "The laptop is loaded with every kind of software you might need as well as the interface into our computer system here at the office. Your password into the computer and into the building after hours is FALCON, all caps."

Startled at the mention of his paratrooper nickname, the one he'd gotten in Jump school, Huck looked up. "Falcon?"

"Just because you aren't the fastest predator in the sky anymore doesn't mean that you aren't still a predator. We're hoping you put those keen skills to work for us here and we don't want you to forget that you've got them." He shrugged. "We thought the name would be a good reminder."

He felt a droll smile roll around his lips. "That sure I would come, were you?"

Payne nodded and the corner of his lip arched in an almost smile. "Yes."

Huck surveyed the employment contract and mentally whistled when he reached his salary. Evidently following his gaze, Payne said, "Top-notch services demand top-end pay. We're confident you'll be worth every penny."

A grim laugh rumbled up Flanagan's throat. "And at the moment, I'm sure McCann would be willing to double your pay."

"What do you say, Huck?" Payne asked. "Are you on board?"

Huck had known the instant Garrett had told him about the offer that he would take the job, but knowing that he'd been *chosen*—that he was still worthy despite his injuries—made him feel infinitely better about it. They'd given him the job on a platter, complete with an apartment and everything else he might need.

In any other case he might have considered it too

good to be true, but in this circumstance he knew better. This was Ranger mentality, a mind-set he completely understood. His gaze bounced back and forth between the two of them and a warm feeling settled in his gut.

It felt…right.

For the first time since his accident, he felt as if he had a place he could belong. Not only would he enjoy working with these men, he instinctively knew they "got" him, just as he instinctively knew they'd always have his back. He was being welcomed into their pack, brought into an elite circle of friends.

Humbled and honored, he picked up the pen lying on the table and scrawled his name across the bottom of the page, then looked up and smiled. "When do I start?"

Flanagan slapped him on the back. "Immediately," he said with a dark chuckle. "Brace yourself, Finn. You're about to *seriously* start earning your pay."

Huck merely grinned. He'd battled terrorists, for pity's sake. He didn't care how damn difficult Sapphira Stravos and her latte-drinking dog were. He knew he could handle her.

"YOUR NEW DETAIL is here, Ms. Stravos," Guy Mc-Cann told her, his voice an unmistakable blend of tight and euphoric.

And she knew exactly how he felt.

Playing the airheaded, self-absorbed spoiled little rich girl was beginning to seriously fray her nerves, but at the same time there was a bit of satisfaction in her victory, shallow though it was.

Over the past week and a half, she'd successfully run off three former Rangers. It had been damn hard work. Truth be told, annoying McCann—who had the least tolerance for bullshit—had been the most fun. Flanagan had muttered curses under his breath, but ever the southern gentleman, he'd merely smiled, gritted his teeth and obliged. Payne had the ice-cold glare down to an art form and, though she knew she'd irritated him as much as she had the others, making him lose the poker face wasn't easy. Familiar with his fortune and hoping to make him a benefactor for Belle Charities at some point in the future, she'd been careful not to push him too far.

No doubt it was his turn again, Sapphira thought, heaving a put-upon sigh for McCann's benefit as she set the fashion magazine she'd been pretending to read aside.

God, this was really beginning to get old.

"Excellent," she said brightly. "I've got several appointments this afternoon and I wouldn't want to get waxed alone."

McCann's self-indulgent smile indicated he thought she was a half-wit. "I think the term you're looking for is 'whacked.'"

"No, it isn't," Sapphira told him, enjoying this entirely too much. "I've seen *The Sopranos*. I know what 'whacked' is. I meant *waxed*. As in brows and bikini area," she added significantly.

His smile fell and a comically blank look, swiftly followed by a darker one, took its place. "I'm sure that Major Finn will keep you safe regardless," he said, his voice almost a growl.

Major Finn? A new guy? she wondered, slightly alarmed. How could that be? There was only supposed to be three of them and she'd already broken them in, so to speak. She'd figured out exactly which buttons to push to drive them crazy—not crazy enough to quit yet, unfortunately, but it was only a matter of time.

Nevertheless, bringing a new guy in certainly cast a fly in the ointment. How was she ever supposed to break them down and make them permanently go away if they kept rotating out long enough to regroup? God help her, how was she ever supposed to get back to work? She couldn't put it off indefinitely and though she had good help in place, there were certain things she preferred to do herself.

Like be there for Carmen. Though she'd missed the last birthing class, she had managed to sneak in a trip to the OB citing "female problems." Even then, Payne had insisted on being right outside the door. What he hadn't known—and what hadn't made it into his report—was that Carmen had already been shown into the room. Regardless of her resourcefulness, she was really growing weary of the whole thing.

She absolutely *hated* being useless, which was exactly what she was at the moment. Honestly, she didn't know how true nonworking heiresses stood it. She'd lose her mind if she had to keep on like this for much longer.

On the heels of that thought, the man she assumed was Major Finn walked into her living room. Impossibly, the force of his presence blasted into her like a sonic boom to her midsection, making her momentarily lose her breath. The fine hairs on the nape of her neck prickled and her mouth parched.

Though reason told her it was impossible, she *felt* him in every cell of her body and the singularly unique reaction left her shaken and unsure.

He was tall and broad-shouldered, much like the other three men of Ranger Security, but she instinctively knew he was different. Playing with him as she had the others would not only be difficult but foolhardy, Sapphira realized through some sort of surreal insight. He was one hundred percent pure testosterone and if there was a weak bone in his body he'd undoubtedly broken it out of spite.

Dark wavy hair—just a shade shy of black—capped his head and showcased a face full of character. She read recklessness in the lean slope of his cheek, which bore a fresh scar, a stubborn streak a mile wide in the hard angle of his jaw, arrogance borne of experience in the thin blade of his nose and absolute fearlessness in those disturbingly keen light gray eyes.

But, ultimately, it was the smile that got her.

Slow, purposeful and just a little irreverent, it unfurled like a bloom over his sinfully beautiful mouth and transformed his face from merely handsome to positively breathtaking. He reminded her of a bird of prey, keen and powerful, agile and quick.

Please be married, please be married, please be married, Sapphira thought, barely resisting the urge to squeeze her eyes tightly shut. If he was married that would make him off limits and she'd have a prayer of controlling this instantaneous attraction she felt spreading through her body like fever. She glanced down at his ring finger and mentally swore.

No ring.

Dammit, she thought, equally thrilled and miserable. Had she found Payne, Flanagan and McCann good-looking? Of course. They were all gorgeous in their own right. But knowing they were married and not experiencing the least bit of attraction to them had left her in a completely different—less vulnerable—position.

Unless this guy had a girlfriend he'd yet to make a bride, she was in serious trouble because she'd never—*never*—seen a man and shivered from the inside out at just looking at him. The tops of her thighs were burning, her belly had given a queer little flutter and her mouth had actually started to water. He was going to be irresistible. She knew it in the same way she knew she couldn't resist plucking the cherry off a banana split or walking past the cookie jar without snagging a ginger snap. Or two.

Quite frankly, he was pure eye candy and she was a self-professed sugarholic, lamentably with a size-fourteen ass to prove it. Unaccountably nervous, she reached for her hand sanitizer again.

"Major Finn, this is Sapphira Stravos," McCann said. "Ms. Stravos, Finn has been briefed, is fully up to speed and ready to assume control here. He will be with you until the threat is neutralized, or hell freezes over, whichever comes first."

Sapphira smiled at him. "I didn't realize we were paying you for sarcasm, Guy," she said, purposely using his first name because she knew it annoyed him. "I'll make sure you're compensated." She felt the cool soothing action of the sanitizer dry on her hands and set the bottle aside.

He snorted. "You'll be receiving an additional bill for Tricky as well."

"It's *Trixie,*" Sapphira said tightly. "As you well know."

Ignoring her, McCann heaved a sigh and slapped her new bodyguard on the back. "I'll owe you a keg at the end of this. Good luck. Trust me, you're going to need it," he added darkly. And with that, he jauntily took his leave.

Rather than respond, Major Finn just smiled, then turned the full force of his attention on her. It took everything she had not to melt beneath the narrow scrutiny of that intense, mesmerizing gaze. She'd never seen eyes that particular shade before. Not precisely blue, not precisely gray, but a subtle mixture in between that put her in mind of a liquid mirror or water over iridescent glass.

In a nutshell, captivating.

"My name is Lucas Finn, but for obvious reasons most people just call me Huck. You're welcome to call me whatever you want, so long as it isn't bastard, son of a bitch or asshole."

Startled, Sapphira felt her eyes widen and she strangled on a laugh. "You get called those often, do you?"

A hint of a smile tugged the corner of his mouth, sending a little cascade of heat tumbling through her sex. "Often enough to issue the warning."

She smiled and extended her hand. "I'm Sapphira. Most people call me Sapphira."

His gaze zeroed in on hers with hawklike accuracy, making the air in her lungs thin to nonexistent. He took her proffered hand and a little earthquake shook her to the soles of her feet. "I'd expected you to have blue eyes."

Used to hearing that, she heaved a little sigh. "Most people do," she said drolly. "But they're green. Occasionally I'll wear the contacts just to meet people's expectations, but frankly, it gets a little old."

"Wearing the contacts or meeting people's expectations?"

Oh, he was too shrewd by half, she thought, reluctantly impressed. "Both."

"You could always give up any pretense and just be yourself," he suggested, once again hitting entirely too close to the mark for comfort. Did they suspect she was hiding something? Sapphira wondered. Had her be-the-biggest-pain-in-the-ass-prima-donna plan backfired? Were they on to her? Maybe, she decided, studying Huck in return. But having suspicions and knowing were two completely different things.

"And you could always stop being a bastard, son of a bitch and asshole and no one would find fault with you, either," she suggested sweetly.

He smiled again, making her pulse trip in her veins. "I could," he acknowledged with a slight nod. Humor danced in that mirrored gaze. "But where's the fun in that?"

Gorgeous *and* wicked. Sweet God, she was doomed.

Please have a girlfriend, Sapphira thought again.

Hell, at this point, even a *boy*friend—as criminally unfair as it might be—would be better than this hot hunk-o-male being a free agent. Unbidden, a vision of his big body hovering over hers, swooping in to kiss her, materialized in her mind's eye. Oh, good grief, Sapphira thought, suppressing a little wail. He was here to protect her, not service her. The fact that she even had to remind herself of that little nugget of insight gave her pause.

Though she'd had lovers over the years, they'd been relatively few and far between. After the miscarriage, she'd been a lot more careful and selective when it came to picking a partner. Frankly, at the time, she'd been more emotionally needy than physically ready for sex. With time and maturity she'd determined that she liked sex and orgasms as much as the next woman, but she'd never been able to give herself to someone she wasn't emotionally invested in or who wasn't at least similarly invested in her. Did she have to be in love? Not precisely. But she had to care about her partner and he had to care for her as well. Call her old-fashioned, but she simply wasn't enough of a progressive thinker to separate the two. Her gaze slid to Huck once more.

Or it hadn't been…until right now.

Clearly the right motivation had never come along.

Clearly she'd never been tested.

Clearly she was in over her head.

Why else would she be staring at this man as if he were the last loaf of bread on the eve of a winter storm? Why else would her body be simmering and trembling, every nerve ending in her being singing as though it had been struck with an electric jolt? Why was she consumed with the insane urge to lick a path up the side of his neck and wrap her arms around his lean waist? Why was she wondering if he tasted like his aftershave—warm and woodsy and thrillingly dark?

Why, why, why?

Evidently she'd lost her mind.

In the space of a few minutes she'd gone from reasonable woman with a purpose to miserable girl with a sudden wretched bone-melting crush.

It was as galling as it was troubling.

"So I've been briefed about the letters and what the agency has recovered about them so far, but I haven't talked to you directly." That disturbingly keen gaze found hers once more, inadvertently sucking the breath out of her lungs. "What are your thoughts? Can you think of any reason anyone would want to hurt you? Are you afraid, or simply irritated that this has disrupted your life?"

Playing the blasé, clueless unconcerned socialite with no more weighty problems than picking out what shoes to wear to the country club might have been easy with the first three men at Ranger Security, but donning the role for this guy was incredibly hard. She wanted to tell him that yes, she was slightly alarmed, but was not afraid. That she didn't have any idea why anyone would want to hurt her, that she doubted the credibility of the letters, and that she thought they were more odd than threatening.

She wanted to say all this and more, then ask him if he had a girlfriend.

In the end, though, after weighing the outcome for all of the people dependent on her income, she dragged on a false smile and gave an airy, unconcerned wave of her hand.

"It's your job to think, Huck," she said with a vacant smile, as though none of it mattered in the slightest. She breezed past him and whistled for Trixie. "Right now I have an appointment."

3

HE'D BEEN WRONG, Huck thought darkly two hours later.

They *weren't* paying him enough.

Sapphira wagged the little dog's paws in his direction as they pulled away from the Pampered Pet Day Spa. "Now, don't those look lovely? I think the hot-pink shade looks *absolutely divine* with her shiny white coat."

Huck snorted, unable to think of a single thing to say that wouldn't be inappropriate considering that, technically, this beautiful but sadly demented woman was his boss. I mean, really, what did one say about a dog getting a pedicure? Better still, what *nice* thing could one say about a dog getting a pedicure?

Honestly, when she'd blown off his question regarding the letters with the announcement about her appointment, he'd assumed she'd needed to go to the doctor, or at the very least something equally important. It never occurred to him—though given the cryptic comments McCann had made about Trixie, in retrospect, it should have—that the appointment was for a spa treatment.

For her dog.

Having grown up on the fringes of the idle rich, Huck knew they could waste an inordinate amount of money on things that were self-indulgent, wasteful and stupid to the point of idiocy, but this—he cast a glance at Sapphira who was currently snuggling her little newly coiffed animal—*this* took the cake.

And to make matters worse, for reasons he couldn't explain, he was jealous of the damn dog.

Odd, too, when he'd been certain that he'd caught a glimpse of…something…behind those surprising pretty green eyes. Though he couldn't put his finger on what exactly, he'd seen it all the same. Longing? Regret? Reticence? A combination of all three, maybe? He couldn't be sure. But something about this was off, Huck decided, every sense he had was on heightened alert, and ultimately, though he could see where it was going to be difficult to keep the goal in focus, his job was to discover precisely what that was.

Furthermore, considering this was his first assignment for Ranger Security, failure simply was not an option. Frankly, he had to live up to their expectations and allowing Sapphira—he cast a dark look at Trixie—or, more disturbingly, her dog to make a fool of him would not happen. He slid them another look and felt his grim mood plummet even further.

Hell would flood, freeze and thaw first.

Of course, in a perfect world she'd be fat, ugly, stupid and unpleasant—she would not have an ass as lush and ripe as a Georgia peach, intelligent eyes the shade of a new leaf on an old vine and a body that put him in mind of hot sex on a hotter night. She would not make his skin burn and his lips twitch and she wouldn't make his dick stir in his jeans. He chalked up that disturbing phenomenon to his recent stint of abstinence—he'd been too busy trying to heal to make sex a priority.

Clearly he'd left it too long, otherwise he was certain he wouldn't possibly be attracted to this woman.

In fact, were there a picture of "Wrong For Me" in his mental dictionary, he was fairly certain Sapphira Stravos's image would be right next to it. Was she pretty? Sexy? Intriguing, even?

Yes to all of the above.

But when the time came for Huck to start thinking about settling down—over even a quick lay—it sure as hell wouldn't be with a woman who thought the best way to spend her money was on a pedicure for her dog. Though admittedly he hadn't given much thought to the future Mrs. Finn—he'd been too busy building a career and frankly, having fun, to consider a permanent relationship—he still knew a wealthy, entitled socialite— the very kind his mother had cleaned up after for years, he thought bitterly—certainly wouldn't fit the bill.

On any level.

No matter how friggin' sexy, he thought as another bolt of heat seared his groin.

Furthermore, he'd yet to meet a woman he'd want to spend more than a couple of nights with, much less the rest of his life, and at thirty, he certainly wasn't in a hurry. Right now mending the train wreck of his life— putting this new career on track—had to be his top priority. And as far as he could see, the only thing standing in the way of that was this little pampered Greek hottie and her equally pampered dog.

Sapphira's lips curled into a mocking smile. "Let me guess. You don't approve."

Huck negotiated a turn, which wasn't easy in her tiny little car, the one she'd insisted that he drive, citing Trixie's familiarity with the vehicle and her penchant for relieving herself in new places. His leg throbbed like a son of a bitch, but he'd eat glass before he'd admit it. Just another example of her thoughtlessness, Huck decided. Her kind were generally only concerned with their own comfort and to hell with everyone else. A patently unfair deduction considering she didn't actually know that his leg ached, but it was easier to dislike her if he took that approach.

And self-preservation, along with the hard-on currently crowding his jeans, told him he *needed* to dislike her.

"It's not my place to approve or disapprove," Huck told her in a voice that didn't encourage conversation. "I'm here to provide protection and expose the source of your threat. That's it. Where to next?" No doubt Trixie was having her teeth bleached or some other such nonsense, Huck thought uncharitably, repressing a grim smile.

Furthermore, though he was sure that it drove her bat-shit crazy, until the issue of her safety was resolved, the most secure place she could possibly be was inside her tidy little cottage on her father's mammoth estate. Mathias Stravos had a top-rate security system. Huck had been given a tour of the grounds as well as apprised of all security systems and protocols on-site before ever being taken directly to his target.

Curiously, while Mr. Stravos was concerned enough to hire additional security for his daughter, he hadn't been concerned enough to speak to her new detail personally. For whatever reason, it struck Huck as very odd. Ranger Security might be the best in the business, but if had been his daughter who was in trouble, he'd want to assess the help personally.

But talk about a surprise, Huck thought, remembering her little house. He was familiar enough with the layout of an estate to know that Sapphira's residence had more than likely been an upper servants' quarters at some point. A nanny perhaps? Odd that she wouldn't live in the mansion with the rest of her family. Come to think of it, though, there wasn't a "rest of the family."

According to the file, her parents were divorced and her only sibling, a brother, had committed suicide four years ago. Was that why she'd moved out of the house? Huck wondered. Had being there alone with her father, who by all accounts was a real hard-ass, been too much for her? Though he'd only seen a small portion of the mansion he had to admit, size notwithstanding, there was a marked difference between the main house and Sapphira's little place.

While certainly furnished with things that were well beyond his price range, the cottage had a warm and cozy feel to it. Almost grandmotherly, for lack of a better description, with large amounts of floral fabric and poofy, overstuffed chairs. Lots of original artwork

decorated the walls—hers? he'd wondered at the time—
and a collection of antique hatpins lined her mantel, all
of them in curious little vases that looked a bit like
ceramic toothbrush holders. Out of all the things she
could collect with a literal fortune at her disposal, it
seemed an odd choice.

Sapphira input the next address into her navigation
system. "Regardless of why you're here, you still have
an opinion. You think it's silly." She lifted her pert nose
into the air, causing the mocha-colored curls around
her face to bounce. "I can tell."

Huck got the distinct impression that she was trying
to goad him into an argument. He knew she couldn't
possibly care what he thought one way or the other
about the dog's beauty regimen. Rather than respond,
he merely ignored her and headed toward their next so-
called appointment.

She heaved a loud sigh. "My, my, aren't you the
conversationalist."

"I am when there's something interesting to talk
about," Huck told her.

"You don't find Trixie interesting?"

He shot a look at the little dog and barely suppressed
a snort of derision. "Not particularly."

"So you don't like animals?"

"I wouldn't say that."

Actually, he'd had a dog—a black Lab named
Blackie (because it was so original)—when he'd been
a boy. Unfortunately, the single military life wasn't con-
ducive to having a pet and he wasn't altogether certain

the life of a security specialist would be, either. If he could find a good sitter, perhaps a pet would be an option. He was suddenly struck with the need to have a dog, a companion, for his new place. Something that he'd chosen, that would be exclusively his. Another warm body in the apartment, one that would be happy to see him when he came home. As soon as he was finished with Sapphira's case he'd get one, Huck decided, curiously buoyed by the decision.

"So your dislike is limited to *my* animal, then?" she asked, irritation tightening her voice.

That settled it, Huck thought. She was definitely trying to pick a fight with him. The important and all too elusive question, of course, was…why? Was she inherently annoying and belligerent or was she merely putting on a special show just for him?

"I haven't spent enough time with Trixie to form an opinion." He slid the dog another glance. "But her taste in nail polish is terrible."

Sapphira's eyes widened and he could have sworn that she almost chuckled. "Terrible?"

Huck shrugged. "Ghastly."

She stared at him. "Ghastly?"

"That's what I said."

She chewed the inside of her cheek. "Why is it ghastly?"

He shot her a wicked smile and said the one thing guaranteed to set her perfectly aligned teeth on edge. "It makes her look cheap."

Rather than breathe fire as he'd expected, a startled

chuckle broke up in her throat. The sound vibrated through him, strummed the back of his spine and pushed a reluctant smile over his lips.

Damn.

"Look here," she said. "You can call my dog lots of things—as a matter of fact, your partner McCann frequently referred to her as the 'spoiled little bitch'— she's delicate, moody, intermittently house-trained, terrified of the vacuum cleaner and will only eat cat food." She paused and pinned him with an imperious glare. "But she is *not* cheap."

Huck felt his lips tremble. "She'll o-only eat c-cat food?"

"That's right." She stroked the little dog's head with reverent protectiveness.

He negotiated a turn and found a parking space at another damn spa, though thankfully this one was intended for humans. "Well, in that case you shouldn't mind what *I've* nicknamed her."

Sapphira paused and her comically suspicious gaze found his. "What have you nicknamed her?"

Another wicked smile curled his lips. "Pussy."

Sapphira listened to Cindy Ward's low whistle as she peered through the crack in the door into the reception area to get a look at Lucas Finn. "I guess it's really tough to be you," her best friend and partner at Belle Charities drawled with a sarcastic smile as she pulled away from the door. She sighed dramatically. "Having to spend *every* minute of *every* day *chained* to that *single good-looking man* out there." Her face blanked. "Poor you."

"Cindy, the fact that he's good-looking and single doesn't negate that I'm still a prisoner and he's the damn guard."

Cindy snuck another peek at Huck. "Oh, and right now he's playing with your Pussy."

"*Cindy!*" Sapphira hissed over her scandalized chuckle, her face flaming. "Keep your voice down." No doubt she'd rue the day she'd shared that little tidbit with her friend. Honestly, it had been all she could do to keep from howling with laughter—after her initial shock, of course—when he'd shared his nickname for her beloved pet. It was crude, crass and unseemly…which was probably why she'd found it so funny. Particularly coming out of that sinfully crafted mouth.

Regardless, she couldn't allow him to refer to Trixie as Pussy. What sort of pet owner would she be if she permitted him to malign her dog that way?

"Would you get back over here and try to focus," Sapphira told her. "I'm running out of time and you haven't finished updating me yet."

Her friend had been too busy wanting the lowdown on Huck to be bothered with the real reason they were sneaking around at the spa doing business under the guise of a pedicure rather than meeting in the inconspicuous offices of Belle Charities as they normally would. Ordinarily Sapphira logged in quite a few hours a week in the office, but given her constant surveillance over the past ten days she'd been in only once.

Considering her every move was being recorded for her father's benefit, she couldn't risk going any more than that and arousing his suspicions. Better to let him— and Huck, though it bothered her more than it should— think that she was more interested in making sure her handbag matched her shoes than whether or not a family had dinner tonight.

Careful not to mess up her toenail polish, Cindy duckwalked back to the chaise lounge. "Oh, all right," she sighed, settling her petite frame onto the chair. "I suppose we've lusted about tall, dark and gorgeous out there long enough."

Sapphira quirked a pointed brow at her friend and applied her hand sanitizer. "We?"

"You might not have been lusting for the past few minutes, but you've been lusting the rest of the time," she said. Her brown eyes twinkled with knowing humor. "I can tell."

That was the problem with having a best friend, Sapphira thought. She could always tell. Sapphira considered her options and decided that the truth would be more efficient. "If I had the time to argue with you about this, I would lie and say no, I don't find him the least bit attractive. However, I don't have time and you aren't going to be satisfied until I confess, so—" Sapphira released a pent-up breath "—yes, I do find him extraordinarily handsome." Mild understatement. If he'd been the cherry on a sundae she would have already devoured him by now. She was hammeringly aware of every move he made—could feel him in her bones—and sweet Lord, she didn't know what sort of cologne the man wore but it absolutely made her want to slither and slide all over him. She bit her lip. "My toes actually curled when he walked into my living room."

Seemingly satisfied, a slow smile slid over Cindy's mouth. "What are you going to do?"

"About what?"

"About *him?*"

She cleared her throat and tried to focus. "I'm going to take the same tack with him that I have with the other three. Wear him down with the empty-headed, vain, shallow heiress routine and hope that he finds out who's sending the letters before Carmen goes into labor."

Cindy's shrewd gaze caught hers and held. "You know that's not what I meant."

She did. Her cheeks puffed as she exhaled mightily. "It's a nonissue, Cindy. He's my bodyguard, for pity's sake." There had to be a conflict of interest in there somewhere, not to mention the fact that her father would have him drawn and quartered.

Furthermore, Sapphira didn't like to date men who were unmanageable, and Lucas Finn had hard to handle written on every beautifully muscled inch of his mouth-watering frame. He reminded her of a big bird, fast and predatory, keen and sinfully forbidding.

"No doubt he could guard the hell out of your body," Cindy said, chuckling wickedly.

Unbidden, an image of Huck's big hands sliding down her bare back, that hot sexy mouth feeding at hers, materialized in her mind's eye, making the air vanish from her lungs. A pulse of heat throbbed between her legs and her palms tingled, aching for the feel of his warm skin beneath her hands. How could she ache for something she'd never had? How could she burn when he hadn't so much as touched her? Better still, how in the hell was she going to mask the attraction if she drooled at the mere sight of him?

Enough, Sapphira thought, forcing herself to focus. "Have you talked to Carmen?"

Cindy nodded. "This morning. She's doing well. Ready to have the baby, but otherwise fine. Her next appointment is on Wednesday at two. She told me to tell you that she'd understand if you couldn't make it."

"Understanding won't keep her from being disappointed," Sapphira told her, letting go a sigh. "I'll have to work something out."

"You've already played the yearly-visit-to-the-gyno card for last week's appointment. How are you going to swing it again so soon with Huck? Tell him you have some sort of VD?"

"Of course not," Sapphira said, shooting her friend a revolted glare. "I'll tell him that one of my tests needs to be redone." Pap smears were notorious for that sort of thing, not that he would have ever heard of one. But if he happened to press the matter—which she sincerely doubted—the explanation sounded authentic enough.

"You could always let me go," Cindy suggested.

"I need you to go where we know I can't," Sapphira reminded her. "You haven't forgotten about the mentoring meeting downtown tonight, have you?"

Cindy made a moue of regret. "No, but I wish you had. I don't like going down there. It's creepy."

She had to admit the inner city after dark gave her a slight pause as well, but the area around Reverend Alton's church was policed quite well. Having been an advocate for the area for years, the reverend had contacted Belle Charities about making donations to his various causes—after-school programs for kids, continuing education for adults and Sapphira's favorite cause, mentoring young unwed mothers.

Her own experience aside, in many cases these girls were virtually alone, with no one to help them become the mothers and providers they would need to be in order to rear a successful, healthy, well-rounded, drug-free child. Though she'd lost her own baby, Sapphira still knew that becoming a mother in the best of circumstances was difficult enough—becoming one with little to no education, spotty nutrition and no help was much worse.

In order to accommodate the growing demand for mentors and firmly believing that one could make a difference, Sapphira had asked for volunteer Belles to become mentors. Like Cindy, many had been nervous about that particular area of town, but ultimately everyone who'd begun to participate had decided the risk was worth the reward.

Naturally Sapphira understood Cindy's reticence—even Ella had been a little worried about her traveling into the inner-city area—but Reverend Alton would ensure her safety and bottom line, as second in command, Cindy had to be there in Sapphira's absence.

"Let's see," Cindy drawled thoughtfully. "You get to go home with that good-looking guy out there and I get to go step over used needles and pray that I don't get mugged—or worse," she added direly with a delicate shudder. "Who's getting the better end of the deal here?"

Sapphira couldn't help but smile. "On the surface you probably think that I am, but let me put it into perspective for you. Yes, I get to go home with that good-looking man out there. But I don't get to touch him or talk to him about anything of importance." She winced. "Instead, I get the happy job of making him think that I am shallow, spoiled, self-absorbed and relatively unintelligent." Her heart drooped a little lower with every unflattering adjective. "Because, at the end of the day, I have to make him dislike me to the point that he quits, or at the very least, asks to be assigned to another case."

Understanding dawned slowly in her friend's intelligent gaze. "And you want him to like you."

"I want everyone to like me," Sapphira said, shifting uncomfortably.

"You didn't care if the other three liked you," she countered. "You didn't like playing the part, but you didn't give a rip whether the other security specialists personally liked you or not." Her gaze narrowed. "What's different about this one?"

Sapphira sighed. "You mean aside from the fact that he made my toes curl? I— I don't know. I just…"

"Like him," Cindy finished, a slow knowing smile curling her lips. "You *like* this one and you don't want him to hate you."

In a nutshell, she supposed that was the truth. She'd never reacted so strongly to a person before in her life— not just physically, which had been disconcerting in and of itself. Sexual attraction aside, there was something more to Lucas Finn, a wounded look behind those curious gray eyes, a sense of sadness lurking beneath that sexy smile. Something haunted him, Sapphira instinctively knew, and the urge to discover his ghosts and exorcise them for him was as strong as her need to breathe. Odd when she'd only been in his company a few hours, but she couldn't deny it all the same. Those issues combined with that rock-your-world smile and I-could-break-you-like-a-twig strength made him lethally appealing.

Unfortunately, ghosts or no, his very presence endangered everything she'd worked so hard to achieve. Too many people were dependent on her to let a little thing like whether or not her bodyguard *liked* her interfere. She had to keep the bigger picture in focus, not just the one he presented.

He had to hate her, Sapphira thought resignedly.

And the sooner the better.

4

"HOW'S IT GOING so far?"

Huck shot a dark look across the lingerie section of the department store and stifled the growing urge to howl. "Fine," he lied into his cell phone, forcing a smile so that maybe it would actually reach his voice. "Everything's going fine."

Jamie Flanagan's low laugh rumbled into his ear. "Bullshit. What? She's got you out shopping with her, doesn't she? I can hear the music. Shoes or panties?"

Huck blinked. "Come again?"

"If she's not carrying the dog to have her hair colored or visiting the gynecologist, then she's either shopping for shoes or looking at panties. The woman can *flat* waste some time in a store and typically, it's one that is designed to make a man miserable."

Huck rubbed the bridge of his nose and squeezed his eyes shut. "It's panties," he admitted, mortified.

He heard Flanagan share that tidbit with the rest of the group and a chorus of you-poor-bastard laughter reached his ears. "S-sorry, man. But better you than me. I served my time. I feel for you."

He felt for himself and he hadn't even reached the end of the first day with her yet. Honestly, she'd been ogling undergarments—slinky, sexy, sheer things held together with tiny bits of lace and thread—for the better part of an hour. He'd watched her disappear into the fitting room, hands loaded down with matching bras and panties and, evidently his imagination was much better than he would have ever dreamed, because he could mentally dress her in each and every matching set with little to no problem at all.

In short—gallingly—his anger wasn't the only thing swelling around here.

Furthermore, though he'd been watching closely, he hadn't seen a single person—aside from the coffee-shop clerk she'd snapped at over the low foam on her latte—who wanted to do her any bodily injury. No sus-picious-looking characters, no threat of any sort. And, though he could have misread the file, he didn't think any of the others had noted anything odd, either.

"Listen, I know I'm the new guy here, but something about this doesn't feel right. For someone who is sup-posedly in danger, she's not the least bit worried and I haven't detected even the slightest hint of a threat."

"We didn't, either," Flanagan admitted. "But the letters are real and her father is worried, so our job is to do what we're getting paid for. Protect her, of course, and find the source of risk."

He knew that—and would follow orders—but it didn't keep him from seriously wondering just what the hell was going on. Another thought struck. "Did you meet her father?"

"No, I didn't. Payne pulled first duty with her and he's the only one who's met Mr. Stravos."

Ranger Security reputation aside, he still thought that was strange.

"Any new developments in the case?" Jamie asked. "Has another letter arrived?"

"Not that I'm aware of. We've, er... We've been gone all day," he admitted. "Pussy had to have her nails painted—

"P-pussy?" Flanagan chuckled. "Isn't the dog named Trixie?"

"It's not what I'm calling her," Huck said grimly. "Then Sapphira had an appointment to get waxed and buffed and *her* nails done." Clearly he'd gone into the wrong business—he needed to open a pet-friendly spa, one where the owners and animals could get their manicures and pedicures, hair and the like done at the same time. The idea made a grim chuckle rise in his throat. He blew out a breath. "Then we had to drive all over town to find a particular shade of lip gloss to match the new nail color 'because the shade at the spa was more peachy than pink.'" Now, *there* was a sentence he never thought he'd use, particularly in the security field. "And now we're here, where she's tried on every freakin' pair of panties in the store, with the exception of the control-top garments."

He glared down at the dog currently resting atop his foot. Meanwhile, he was dog-sitting. Again.

Jamie laughed once more, then apologized. "Sorry, man. We warned you."

Yes, they did. Regardless, this was not at all what he'd envisioned when he'd signed on for the job. Naturally he hadn't expected anything to be so thrilling as being a paratrooper—free-falling through the sky was a singularly unique sensation, which he knew from personal experience had no rival, and God, how he missed it—but he *had* expected to need adrenaline more than patience, at the very least.

"You're not regretting your decision, are you?" Flanagan asked, showcasing a keen sense of insight.

When he'd rather not lie, Huck had learned to merely remain silent.

Flanagan let go an uneasy breath. "Look, if it makes you feel any better, in three years of business this is the first case we've had of this sort."

"Hopefully it'll be the last," Huck told him, resisting the urge to rub his throbbing leg. At any rate, what did it matter? He couldn't be a paratrooper anymore and this was the best gig in town. Even if it didn't feel like it at the moment, Huck thought, staring morosely at the checkout counter where Sapphira had finally moved.

Promising to call with regular updates, he disconnected. He'd barely stowed the phone in the holder before it vibrated. Huck checked the caller ID display and felt a smile tug the edge of his mouth. Mick.

"How's it going, Falcon? You teaching those boys how to kick some security ass yet?"

Huck chuckled. "Hardly. I'm guarding a socialite and we're presently in the panty section of a department store."

Mick's easy laugh came over the line. "She pretty?"

That would be the first thing his hell-raising love'em-and-leave'em friend would ask. "Did you hear me?" Huck asked, purposely ignoring the question. "I'm in a *panty* department."

"Yeah, well, I'm getting ready to head out again."

Huck's senses went on point. "Where?"

"You know I can't say. Just another miserable village in another war-torn country."

He detected an unusual undercurrent in his friend's voice—reticence? Fear? "When will you be back?"

"End of the week, God willin'."

"Be careful."

Mick laughed. "When you're as good as I am, you don't have to be careful."

Arrogant bastard, Huck thought, shaking his head. "You're so full of shit."

"And you're in a panty department, guarding a pretty woman. Wanna trade?"

Huck's gaze homed in on Sapphira. "I never said she was pretty."

"I know. Sometimes it's what goes unsaid that ends up being the most telling."

"What? Have you been reading your fortune cookies again?"

"Asshole," Mick retorted, laughing. He paused. "Have you heard anything from that P.I. you hired?"

Mick was the only person on the planet who knew

why he'd buggered that training session, who knew that he'd decided he had to find out who his father was. He swallowed. "He called this morning. He still doesn't have anything yet, but he's working on it. It's tough going because Red Rock is a small town and I don't want my mother to know that I'm doing any snooping around."

"I still think you need to just ask her."

He knew what his friend thought and he disagreed. He just couldn't bring himself to do it. He was too afraid of hurting her. "You know I don't want to do that."

"If you want answers, you may end up not having a choice."

Huck sighed. He'd just have to cross that bridge when he came to it. He told Mick as much. "Give me a call when you get back, will you?" It was the closest thing to a let-me-know-you're-okay as he could get.

"Will do," Mick told him, accepting the gesture for what it was. Huck disconnected, thankful that Mick had been a stubborn son of a bitch and hadn't given up on him as a friend after the accident. He smiled. Oh, hell. Who was he kidding? When had he ever known Mick Chivers to give up on anything? Belatedly remembering his target, Huck's gaze found Sapphira once more.

Is she pretty?

Though he'd ignored his friend's question, the query came back to haunt him. In the traditional sense, no, she wasn't what one would call pretty. Her face was a little too round, her nose a little too pert. Her mouth, though, was possibly the most beautiful thing he'd ever seen.

Extra-full bottom lip, bowed upper, and wide enough to make him hard.

The overheard light gleamed over the caramel highlights in her pale brown hair, and her tiny foot, clad in a shoe that would more than likely cover the monthly food bill for the average family of four, tapped in time with the beat of the piped-in music. She wore a pair of red butt-hugging capri pants that clung to her ripe rear end with just enough cling to be a degree shy of tight and a white scoop-necked T-shirt with lots of little sparkly doodads. She looked funky but chic and sexy as hell.

She turned then, and smiled at him—and just like that the breath that had been in his lungs silently evaporated, as though it had magically disappeared.

Oh, hell, Huck thought as his mouth parched and his heart rate kicked up a notch. Another blast of heat landed in his loins and he resisted the urge to gnash his teeth and scream.

This was *so* not good.

On too many levels to count.

"I'm ready," she said brightly, shoving her newest purchases at him as though he was her personal bag boy. It was like a welcome splash of cold water over his privates. Though it went against every bit of southern-gentleman training he'd received from his mother and grandmother, Huck made himself stand still and not accept her load.

Seemingly stunned, she stared blankly at him. "Aren't you going to carry these for me?"

"Did you buy them for me?"

She smirked. "I wasn't aware that you were into that sort of thing." Her gaze slid over him and she cocked her head in exaggerated bewilderment. "Just goes to show you can never tell." She leaned forward conspiratorially. "Tell me, are you wearing a bra now?" she stage-whispered to everyone within a fifty-foot radius, much to his immediate discomfort.

Lips pursed into a thin line, he grabbed her arm and propelled her out of the store. Trixie yelped into action. "You know damn well I don't wear a bra."

"How would I know that?" she asked, hurrying to keep up with him. "For all I know you've got on a thong, too."

He felt his teeth almost crack. "I can assure you that I don't have on a thong."

Eyes twinkling, she slid him a provokingly sly grin. "But you won't assure me you're not wearing a bra?"

"I'm not wearing a bra, either," he clarified through a tight smile. "And while we're on the subject of what I'm *not* doing, maybe I should take this opportunity to clarify a few things for you." He drew up short and whirled her around to face him, then glared down into her irritatingly sensual face. "I'm *not* going to dog-sit or tote your bags. I'm *not* going to fetch the sugar for your coffee or select the color of your nail polish." He felt his expression blacken as another pain sliced through his leg. "And I'm *not* going to drive your car anymore. In fact, if I let you leave the house again—and at the moment that's a pretty big if—we're taking my car and you're sitting in the—"

Huck paused as sudden inspiration, like a gilded gift

from the heavens, descended upon him. He felt a smile slide slowly, wonderingly, over his lips.

Alarm registered in those startling green eyes. "What do you mean if you let me leave the house?" she asked, growing pale.

"That's exactly what I mean," Huck told her, laughing softly as the brilliance of the idea—the solution to his problem—unfurled in his furious mind. That was it. That was the key. Honestly, he didn't know why Payne, Flanagan and McCann hadn't thought of it.

His gaze slid to hers and caught. He'd put her in lockdown mode. Hadn't he just thought she was safer at home than out in public? That her father's compound was the best possible place for her to be? No more running around feeling foolish. No more beauty appointments and shopping.

Hell, it would probably be good for her. She could read a book or something, he thought uncharitably.

"You'd better get your errands done today, sweetheart, because your days of leading me around like a circus bear are over. Starting tonight, you're going under house arrest."

She gasped, then her eyes narrowed and the intelligence he'd glimpsed off and on all day suddenly flared in those green orbs. "The hell I am."

"I think perhaps you have confused me with your other hired help," Huck pointed out. "*I* don't have to follow *your* orders. *You* have to follow *mine*."

Impossibly, her eyes narrowed further. "Listen, Jack. I don't work for you. You work for—"

"Your father," Huck interjected. "And the name's not Jack. It's Huck."

She glared up at him. "I'm beginning to see why the son of a bitch, bastard and asshole nicknames followed you around. And my father—"

"Will follow my recommendation," he finished for her, once again cutting her off. From her mutinous expression it was a novel experience for her, and for reasons which escaped him, it made this moment all the more enjoyable.

He *liked* pissing her off. It was fun.

"He's paying for my professional opinion, and the instant we get back I'm going to give it to him." He chuckled darkly. "Unless it's an emergency of epic proportions, your newly waxed, buffed and painted ass isn't leaving the house. Playtime is over, sweetheart."

HE COULDN'T POSSIBLY be serious, Sapphira thought as a triumphantly smiling Huck held the car door open for her. He might have been doing it out of courtesy, but it felt as if he was ushering her into a jail cell, or worse still, the last walk for a death-row inmate. Panic punched her heart rate into overdrive and nausea spun in her suddenly churning gut.

House arrest? *House arrest?*

Had he lost his freaking mind?

No, dammit, she was the one who'd lost her mind. She'd known—*known*—the instant she'd laid eyes on him that he was different, that he wouldn't put up with her the way that the others had. She'd recognized it, but hadn't changed her tack, hadn't developed a new strategy.

She watched him round the car, a slight limp to his gait, and observed the faintest hint of a wince behind the grin he wore at her expense. She'd noticed the hitch in his step this morning when she'd first met him, but couldn't recall seeing it the rest of the day. Come to think of it, though, he'd either been sitting in the car, in a chair, or leaning against the wall.

As he angled into her tiny car and wedged himself behind the wheel, a bolt of insight flashed in her otherwise preoccupied mind and she inwardly squirmed with shame. Clearly piloting her Mini Cooper hadn't helped with whatever ache pained his leg. Ordinarily she wasn't so dim and thoughtless, but the sight of him earlier today and his overall appearance had rattled her beyond the usual measure. Her guardian bird of prey obviously had a broken wing, she thought, shooting him a look from the corner of her eye.

"I can be reasonable," Sapphira said, dragging her shredded thoughts together and forcing herself to remain calm. "If driving my car hurts your leg, then we can take yours. Why didn't you say something?"

She watched his jaw tighten as he shifted gears and expertly merged into traffic. "Who said anything about my leg hurting?"

"Nobody had to say anything. It's obvious. You've got a bit of a limp."

"I'm not making you stay home because of any physical discomfort on my part," he all but growled. "It's a safety issue."

Sapphira rolled her eyes. "Bullshit. You just don't

like following me around. News flash, Huckleberry, that's your job."

He slid her a look that would have wilted steel and frightened small children. "My job is to protect you, not follow you around. Contrary to popular belief, they aren't synonymous."

"Then why didn't the others balk?"

He snorted. "They were too nice." He bared his teeth in another disturbingly thrilling smile, and those mesmerizing eyes pinned her to her seat. "I am not."

Her muddled belly did a little roll and, against all sense, her nipples tingled at the blatantly bald comment. Sweet God, what was wrong with her? The man was being a complete ass—and an obstinate one at that—and yet she found herself curiously aroused.

Clearly the heat from the unusually potent attraction had fried her brain, otherwise she was certain she'd give him a real piece of her mind, not the dumbed-down version she'd been sharing with the other men over the past week and a half.

Sapphira looked away and harrumphed under her breath. "Trust me, it's nothing to be proud of."

"That's a matter of opinion."

"That's right. *Mine,*" she added pointedly.

A low chuckle rumbled up his throat. "And I suppose you think yours is the only one that matters?"

"Of course not," she snapped, annoyed despite the fact that she'd obviously given him that impression. At the moment it felt like a very shallow victory. "But if you think you're going to keep me locked up until you figure out who's sending those ridiculous letters, then you'd better think again." She pulled out her hand sanitizer and squirted a dollop onto her right palm, then put her hands together and gave them a vicious rub. "I have things to do."

He grunted. "Your spray-on tan can wait."

Sapphira felt her mouth drop open. "I don't—and have *never*—gotten a spray-on tan," she said through tightly gritted teeth.

Obviously having watched her apply the hand gel, he jerked his head in her direction. "What's with the disinfectant stuff? You've been putting it on all day."

"I've been touching things covered with germs all day," she retorted. "Did you know that some bacteria and viruses can live for up to two hours on a doorknob?"

A smile caught the corner of his mouth. "Er…no, I didn't."

She hadn't, either, until she'd watched that primetime special. At first she'd just been appalled at the number of people who didn't wash their hands after using the restroom and had decided that hand sanitizer was a good way to combat other people's uncleanly behavior, but once she'd started using the gel… Well, suffice it to say, it was more addiction now than habit. She craved that cool feeling on her palms. She kept multiple bottles in her purse and around her house. She needed it. Without it, she could practically feel the germs crawling all over her hands.

"Well, they do." She held the bottle out to him. "Want some?"

"No, thanks. What makes you think the letters are 'ridiculous'?"

Dammit, she was going to have to be more careful. She should have known he'd pick up on that slip. "They're ridiculous because they are disrupting my life," she said, exasperated and thankful it was, in part, the truth. "I have things to do."

Huck presented ID at the gate, then pulled around to her house. "Yes, well, that list just got shortened considerably. From this point forward all of your errands will be vetted by me and I will decide whether or not they are pressing or can wait until we've determined the source of your threat."

"Well, just exactly what have *you* done about that?" Sapphira asked, feeling panic fuel her ascending blood pressure. "Could you tell me what *you've* done to find out who's sending me the damn letters?"

Huck shifted into park and immediately climbed out of the car to stretch. Rather than wait on him to round the hood and open her door, Sapphira scrambled out as well. "Well?" she demanded. She knew she was being unfair and unreasonable. The man had scarcely been on the job eight hours and she'd had him chauffeuring her around the majority of that time. She knew she was being a certified pain in the ass, but couldn't seem to help herself. Her life was spinning out of control and she seemed utterly powerless to stop it.

And for whatever reason, *he* seemed to be making things worse. His presence, his attitude, not to mention this crazy attraction. Truth be told, she'd offered him the hand gel to see if she could eliminate a bit of that strangely wonderful scent that seemed to ooze out of his pores.

Furthermore, she'd caught the disgusted look on his face when she'd snapped at Mark, the coffee clerk, and the realization that her plan to make him dislike her was working had left her more depressed than happy. Did he know that she'd slipped Mark a hundred dollars last week to play along? That she'd apologized in advance for her tacky behavior so that he wouldn't be hurt that she'd suddenly turned into a screaming harpy from hell?

No. He didn't. And couldn't ever know it. Otherwise her plan, such as it was, would be ruined.

And as far as a plan went, she had to admit it was pretty stupid. Entertaining at times, but ill conceived, ineffective and ignorant. Had she annoyed them? Made them miserable?

Certainly.

But she hadn't managed to permanently put them off and knew that, ultimately, she wouldn't be able to pull that sort of coup. These men were former Rangers, for pity's sake. Bona fide badasses. They'd been put through some of the most rigorous military-training exercises in the known world and had come through on the other end. They were modern-day warriors, Uncle Sam's elite, the cream of the crop. Had she honestly believed that being a shallow prima donna with more money than sense would really make them go away? Quit, even?

She inwardly sighed. Who was she kidding? They weren't going anywhere. Her gaze slid to Huck. And he sure wasn't. He would ride it out regardless because he was just that damn stubborn.

And only she would find that deeply sexy. She smothered a whimper and resisted the urge to howl with frustration.

"What have I done to locate the letter writer?" Huck asked, glaring wide-eyed at her from across the hood. "You know very well what I've done today, princess. I haven't had time to piss," he said, glowering at her, "much less investigate who wants to hurt you. Though given the day that we've had together I can see that the suspect list should include anyone in the food service, retail sales and personal-hygiene industries."

The jibe, while deserved, struck a nerve.

"But you can rest assured we won't have another repeat of today." He paused and shot her a shrewd look with those clear gray eyes. "We're done playing by your rules. From now on we're following mine. And, believe me," he added, laughing softly, though it lacked any genuine humor, "no one wants to neutralize the threat more than I do."

Meaning, he couldn't wait to get away from her.

Mission accomplished, girl genius, she thought, her heart sagging as Trixie did her pee-pee dance around her leg. And in record time, too. *He hates you.*

It should have been the least of her worries, but oddly enough…it wasn't.

5

"I UNDERSTAND THAT Sapphira isn't going to like being
confined, sir, but under the circumstances I think it's our
best bet for keeping her safe until we've uncovered the
source of the letters."

Mathias Stravos, a remote robust sixty-something
with tanned skin and a full head of bristly salt-and-
pepper hair, didn't respond at first. The man was too
busy staring at his computer screen to offer any sort of
reply. And had been since the moment Huck had been
granted entrance into his opulent office. "Damn tech-
nology," he muttered, poking angrily at the keyboard.
"Why can't this thing run any faster?"

Given the way he'd been abusing the machine, Huck
thought it was a miracle the computer hadn't fallen
apart already. Stravos had been slapping the side of the
monitor as though it were a vending machine with a
stuck snack. He inwardly grimaced. Not exactly the
best way to handle delicate equipment. Clearly, finesse
and patience weren't part of his character makeup.

Quite frankly, for reasons he didn't know but trusted
nonetheless, he didn't like the man. He was arrogant,

entitled and cold. Had he always been that way? Or had his son's suicide precipitated the change?

Whatever the case, he hadn't been able to miss the flash of fear he'd caught in Sapphira's eyes when he'd announced his intention to go and talk with her father. What exactly was she afraid of? Huck wondered, intrigued. Her father? After meeting the man he could certainly see why she'd find him intimidating, but fear? It was all very strange.

"I hired your company to protect my daughter. If I wanted to make her a prisoner I would have confined her myself."

And no doubt he could have done it as well, Huck thought, oddly chilled. He'd gotten a strange vibe regarding Sapphira's father from the moment he arrived, but now that same premonition was ringing so hard he could feel it rattling his spine.

"I'm not talking about making her a prisoner," Huck felt compelled to point out, his tone even and firm. "I'm talking about keeping her safe. Taking the dog to the groomer, in my opinion, is an unnecessary risk until we've isolated the threat. Furthermore, it's hard to focus on the investigation if I'm chaperoning a shopping trip. Frankly it's an unwarranted hazard and a waste of my time and your money." He shrugged, unconcerned. He sure as hell wasn't afraid of him. "However, if you want me to continue—"

"No, no," he interrupted impatiently, once again whacking the computer. The man had yet to look him in the eye, an indirect insult and overall lack of respect.

"That won't be necessary. All trips out of the compound are at your discretion. I'll see to it that Sapphira doesn't give you any trouble." Huck didn't detect the slightest bit of fatherly affection in the man's voice and it put him instantly on guard on Sapphira's behalf. Why? Who the hell knew? But it was a gut-check reaction and he knew better than to ignore it.

"That won't be necessary. I don't anticipate her giving me any trouble."

At that, Stravos finally looked up and a flash of unreadable emotion washed over his lined face. "Then you obviously don't have children, otherwise you would know that they are nothing but trouble." His gaze drifted over to a photograph on his desk, presumably of his son, and grew shuttered. "Good evening, Mr. Finn. I'll expect daily reports of your progress."

Summarily dismissed, Huck stood and made his way out, thankful that the bizarre meeting was over. At any rate, he'd accomplished what he'd set out to do, which was putting an end to Sapphira's ridiculous running around. While the local economy might take a little hit, he considered it a public service. The unkind thought made him smile, but he'd had so little pleasure today he'd take it where he could get it.

Honestly, he didn't know when he'd ever met anyone quite like her. For the majority of the day she'd been a monumental pain in the ass, but occasionally he'd caught an unmistakable glimpse of intelligence and humor lurking behind those interesting green eyes, shaping the curve of that kissable mouth.

One he'd looked at entirely too much over the course of their afternoon.

She had the most expressive face, Huck thought, reluctantly intrigued. How many times had he watched her lift that little chin? Those lips tremble with a smile? Her eyes widen in outrage or narrow in irritation? And she had this way of barely cocking her head in bewilderment that, to his horror, he found absolutely adorable.

Kittens were adorable, dammit.

And she was no kitten.

In fact, the only thing catlike about her was that sultry feline smile that made him think of warm breath and puckered nipples, of welcoming thighs and a shadowed belly button. He paused on the path back to her house and swore, waiting for the fire in his loins to subside.

Things he definitely shouldn't be thinking about— particularly with her.

Huck looked toward her house and saw her through the tall windows that marched across the front of her Greek Revival cottage. Despite the balmy heat, she'd opened the shutters, and white gauzy curtains fluttered in the evening breeze. A ceiling fan swirled overhead, blowing strands of mocha-colored hair around her face. She sat curled up in a chair, the phone pressed to her ear. Her face was an exasperated mask of worry and irritation. The irritation he understood—he'd caused it. But the worry…

It was genuine.

She wasn't worried about the threatening letters, but *was* worried about not going to the beauty parlor or to the mall? Surely not, Huck thought. Despite all the evidence to the contrary today, he knew she had a deeper character than that. The question was…why was she trying to hide it?

His cell vibrated at his waist. "Finn," he answered.

McCann laughed into his ear. "You are a friggin' *genius*. I'm lifting a longneck in your honor right now."

Confused, Huck chuckled and passed a hand over his face. "Thanks, but I'm afraid I don't follow."

"Putting Princess Pain in the Ass under house arrest," he all but crowed. "Brilliant, my man. Simply brilliant."

He frowned. "How did you know—"

"She called a few minutes ago and asked Payne to come back. She told him that you were an 'insufferable boorish clod' and she *could not* deal with you."

Huck glared at her through the window, then set off at a faster clip toward her house. He made a point of stomping up the steps to alert her of his presence. "Oh, really?" he asked, pushing into the room. Sapphira scrambled to get off the phone and shot him another inconvenienced grimace. "An insufferable boorish clod? That's certainly a new one," he drawled, pinning her with his gaze. He stalked purposely toward her.

He had the privilege of watching a blush spread up her neck and over her cheeks.

"Aside for asking for a replacement, did she say anything else?"

"Just that you'd put her under house arrest and she couldn't work with you, that one of us would have to return. Payne was very diplomatic in that he didn't tell her we'd all rather have our nuts exposed to a flesh-eating virus first." He chuckled darkly. "He just told her that the three of us were busy with other clients and that she would simply have to 'make do.' That if you thought she was safer within the compound she should respect your opinion."

Huck snorted. "I'll bet that went over like a lead balloon."

"She wasn't happy, no. What did her father say? She'd said you'd gone to talk to him."

"Her father agreed with me and said he would make sure that Sapphira didn't give me any trouble."

No doubt about it, Huck thought as he watched another shadow move over her eyes. That was fear.

Intrigued, he studied her for a moment, searched her face for any more clues. "I told him that wouldn't be necessary, that I was perfectly capable of making sure she stayed in line."

"No doubt you can handle her," McCann said, seemingly impressed. "You've sure as hell done a better job of dealing with her than we did. Have I mentioned how glad I am that you've joined our team?"

Huck smiled. "It's not feeling like a team at the moment, McCann. More like every man for himself."

Guy laughed. "Yeah, well. It is what it is. We'll work our end and you work yours."

"You got it." He disconnected and stared down at her, waiting for her to say something.

She didn't. Just glared at him with an embarrassed but mutinous expression.

"You asked for a replacement?" he said, practically

chewing the words. Throttling her was beginning to look really good. Granted, her phone call had gone in his favor, but...

"You tattled to Daddy?" she retorted.

"I didn't *tattle* to your father—I apprised him of the new developments."

"Call it what you want, Huck, it was still a shitty thing to do." She shoved her hair out of her face. "I'm not twelve, dammit."

He pulled a shrug, conveniently ignoring the truth of her statement. Talking to Stravos had been a bit like ratting her out, but truth be told, he'd really just wanted to meet the man and get a feel for him. "Then act like it," he told her.

She shot him another dirty look, then abruptly stood and muttered something that sounded suspiciously like a "fuck you." Though he should have been offended, he had to smother a smile.

"Where are you going?" he asked as she headed for the door.

"To eat. I'm hungry."

"Me, too. What are we having?"

"I'm having Ella's red beans and rice." She smiled sweetly. "You can eat shit."

"Honestly, child, you can't expect me to let the man sit in my house but not have anything to eat," Ella chided moments later as Sapphira loaded her plate full of the steaming Cajun dish Ella had made for their dinner. "It's unkind."

"Who said he had to sit in the house?" she asked. "You've got a perfectly good swing on the front porch."

Small but strong, Ella paused and considered her with those wise blue eyes. "You didn't mind if the other three put their feet under my table. Why can't this one?"

Sapphira harrumphed, still annoyed. She plopped down into her chair and squeezed a wedge of lemon into her sweet tea. "This one has put me under house arrest."

Ella started. "What?"

"Starting tomorrow, I can't leave the house unless he approves of the errand. I have to have his friggin' *permission* to leave."

"Language, Sapphira," she scolded, her brow wrinkling. Her eyes suddenly twinkled and a knowing smile curled her lips. "I take it this one didn't like all the shopping and whatnot."

"The other ones didn't like it, either, but they did it."

Ella made a little *hmmph*. "All that says to me is that this one is smarter than the rest."

Outraged, Sapphira's eyes widened. "Ella, how can you say that? He's making me a prisoner!" she hissed.

"No, he's not. He's clipping your wings. Frankly, after the heck you put the others through, I think it's no less than you deserve."

Sapphira felt her shoulders droop. "If I wasn't so hungry I'd lose my appetite." She picked at a piece of rice with her fork. "You're supposed to be on my side."

"I am on your side, child," she soothed. "If you remember, I never agreed with your 'solution' to get rid of your bodyguards."

That was putting it mildly. Ella had thought her PITA plan, aka pain in the ass agenda, had been "pure rubbish." She'd never approved. Still, was a little support from her dearest friend too much to ask for? Having Huck screen all of her errands was seriously going to cramp her already twisted style. How was she supposed to take care of her duties for Belle Charities? Mentor? Be there for Carmen? She'd skimmed the reports McCann, Payne and Flanagan had submitted to her father. Other than bathroom breaks, they accounted for every minute of her day. If she went about her normal routine, her father would cut her off so quick her head would spin.

And then what?

What would all of the people dependent on her help do? Her so-called salary helped feed families, covered health insurance. There was nothing frivolous about *those* expenditures, dammit, regardless of what Huck thought about her dog having her nails painted.

Honestly, at this point, Sapphira didn't know what to do. Going about business as usual wasn't an option. Confronting her father wasn't an option. Her only hope at this point was that the letters would stop coming and her father would decide to remove her security detail.

Then and only then would she have her life back.

"Mr. Finn," Ella called. "Would you like to join us?"

Huck appeared in the doorway so fast it was almost funny. He smiled at Ella. "Thank you, I would." He took the seat opposite her. "It smells wonderful."

"Aw, it's just a little red beans and rice," Ella said, blushing at the praise.

Damn charmer, Sapphira thought, feeling her toes curl into her shoes. Despite the aromatic dish, she could smell Huck above the food, that same woodsy, musky scent that had been driving her insane all day. Furthermore, though she was exhausted—and knew he had to be as well, because nothing wore a body out faster than good old-fashioned boredom—Huck, damn him, seemed sharp. The limp she'd noticed earlier had vanished, probably from sheer force of will, Sapphira decided, inwardly impressed.

She knew she'd struck a nerve when she'd mentioned it, and could tell the ache was more than just physical. His soul was wounded as well. What had happened to him? she wondered. Was the new scar on his cheek related to the leg injury? As a former Ranger, had he been wounded in action? Or had it been something as unfortunate as a car accident? For reasons that escaped her, she suddenly *had* to know. Of course, considering she'd just told the man to eat shit, he probably wasn't interested in confiding close personal details about himself to her, Sapphira thought, inwardly smiling.

Ever the southern hostess, Ella loaded Huck's plate and filled his glass, then set both down in front of him. Thirty seconds later the only sound was the scrape of a fork against a plate.

Huck hummed impressively under his breath. "Ms. Ella, this is wonderful. Thank you."

"You're welcome. Sapphira and I usually eat supper together, so feel free to join us anytime. There's always plenty." She paused. "That's a southern accent. What part of the South are you from?"

He took a sip of tea. "I'm from Georgia as well—Red Rock. Just a bit west of Savannah."

"I've heard of Red Rock," Ella said. "Sweet little town. You've got family there?" She wasn't being nosy, merely polite, which Huck seemed to recognize because, after darting her a look, he answered Ella's question.

"Just my mom and grandmother," he said casually, though she did notice that his fingers tightened around his fork. "My mother was a maid for years, but has since opened a cookie bakery. If I'm still here on Friday, I'll share a few with you. She sends a care package every week," he confided. "My grandmother is a retired seamstress. She and my mom recently moved to Savannah."

His mother had been a maid? Sapphira thought, surprised. If she'd been treated unfairly, then that could certainly account for a bit of the disdain she'd picked up on. And no mention of a father? Another telling omission she filed away for future reference.

Sapphira smiled. "A cookie bakery? Really? I've always wished that I could bake."

"Don't let her fool you," Ella chimed in with a knowing chuckle. "Sapphira knows her way around the kitchen, she just doesn't like to eat alone."

That disturbingly intuitive gaze slid to hers and caught. He didn't say a word and yet she knew what he was thinking, could tell he wanted to know why she ate with Ella instead of her father. Sapphira quirked a pointed brow at him, daring him to ask. *Go ahead, Huck. Then I'll ask about* your *father and see how you like it.*

"Really?" he said after a slight pause. "I'll have to see

if I can get her to cook something for me." He winced thoughtfully. "Of course, there's always the chance that she'd season it with arsenic, so I'd better not."

Ella chuckled and Sapphira felt a reluctant laugh bubble up her own throat as well. "No doubt you'd survive," she said. "Roaches are like that, too."

Huck's eyes twinkled at the insult and he chewed the corner of his mouth. "You're in fine form tonight. Are you always this pleasant?"

She batted her lashes at him. "I'm making a special effort just for you."

He laughed again, seemingly startled at her candor. "Somehow I figured as much. Try not to tax yourself too much though, because if you break a nail you're not going to get it repaired." Much to her irritation, he delivered the remark with a pointed grin.

"Ah, back to my incarceration, are we?"

"Sapphira, Mr. Finn is merely doing his job," Ella said, the ever-present voice of reason. "He's trying to keep you safe."

Sapphira darted him a perturbed look. "Yeah, but he's enjoying it a little too much."

He shrugged, trying once again not to smile. That sensual mouth curved ever so wickedly around the edges. "You make it so easy."

Ella's shrewd gaze bounced between them consideringly. "Have you had any luck determining the source of the letters?" she asked.

"Not yet. But we will," he added confidently.

Sapphira made a doubtful moue because she knew it

would annoy him. "I tell ya, at this point I'm just hoping the letters stop so that my guards are released and I'm a free woman again."

He ignored the jibe. "How long has it been since the last one? A week?"

"Yes. I'm going to give it a couple more days, but if I don't get another letter, I think I can convince my father to suspend your services."

Ella harrumphed. "I'm surprised he hired anyone to start with."

Sapphira watched Huck's gaze sharpen and once again he reminded her of a disturbingly large bird of prey. "Oh?" he prodded.

"Ella," Sapphira cautioned with a dark look.

"He's met your father," she said. "It's no secret that he doesn't like being inconvenienced. He should have been the one looking into this for you. But can he be bothered? No," she said, clearly irritated. She shook her head and tsked under her breath. "That man lost his soul when Nicky died, and I've about given up hope that he'll get it back."

It was true, Sapphira knew. Her father had never been particularly affectionate when she'd been growing up, but there had been moments when she'd known she was loved. In all honesty, she couldn't say she'd felt so much as a brush of affection from him since Nicky passed away. Her gaze slid to Huck, who'd gone quiet. He knew about her brother, she was sure. They all did. It would have been in any background research they'd done on her family.

"I'm sorry about your brother," he finally said. "That must have been tough."

Tough didn't begin to cover it, Sapphira thought as her heart ached anew with the loss. In a home with two distant parents, she and Nicky had depended a lot upon each other. They'd been close. Honestly, when she'd first heard the news that he'd overdosed, the burst of anger over his leaving her—not confiding in her—was almost more potent than the grief.

A coping mechanism, her therapist had told her when she'd gone in for counseling. Whatever, Sapphira thought. In the end, none of the labels or terminology had mattered. Her only brother was gone and she was left in a world that didn't feel particularly right without him.

Sapphira stood and collected her plate. "Let me help you clear the dishes," she said, suddenly exhausted.

Ella made a noise of protest and took the dish out of her hand. "Another time, child. You go on home. You look a bit tired."

Sapphira smiled down into Ella's lined face, affection welling from deep within her chest. Oh, how she loved Ella. What on earth would she do without her? "Are you sure?"

"Of course." She leaned in, smiled and jerked her head in Huck's direction. "And you be nice," she admonished.

Sapphira chuckled wearily under her breath and pressed a kiss against Ella's cheek. "I'll try."

It was only when they'd walked outside and started down the path back to her house that Sapphira realized a whole new problem was about to begin.

Lucas Finn—all six and a half feet of him, every wonderfully proportioned sex-on-feet inch—was going to be spending the night with her. Indefinitely even. And the only advice her ordinarily levelheaded, conservative former nanny had to offer was "be nice."

She whimpered as his arm brushed hers and that mesmerizing scent once again teased her nostrils. Her body did a little simmer and every nerve ending vibrated with what she tried to tell herself was irritation.

It wasn't.

Irritation didn't make her nipples tingle and her sex sing. Irritation didn't make her want to slide all over him. Irritation didn't make her want to taste the lingering flavor of red beans and rice on his sinfully beautiful mouth. Irritation didn't make her want him. She stifled another moan as they walked through her door. The two of them. Alone in her house. In the dark of night. For hours on end.

God help her.

6

GEEZ GOD, how long did it take to shower? Huck wondered helplessly as the continued noise—and the ensuing vision of hot naked skin, wet and supple and welcoming—plagued him. Though he was probably sitting on a mattress—under the guise of reading because he sure as hell couldn't sleep—that cost more than his entire bedroom suite, he couldn't get comfortable. He chuckled miserably.

Hard to get comfortable when he had a blazing erection from hell straining against his shorts.

Because of her.

He seriously couldn't believe that his body was doing this to him, betraying him to a pampered little rich girl who more than likely didn't have a clue how the other half lived. How women like his mother had struggled to keep a roof over their heads, food on the table and clothes on their backs by constantly cleaning up after someone else.

Huck knew he painted her with a broad brush, but he couldn't seem to help himself. If he didn't keep reminding himself of all her faults and unfairly stereotyping her into a neat little box, he was horribly afraid he'd snap and do something, if not unforgivable, then at least unforgivably stupid.

Like *like* her.

And if he liked her, he'd seduce her.

And that… He shifted miserably, felt a single bead of moisture leak from his dick. Well, that was just too ignorant to comprehend.

Though it took every available brain cell, Huck forced himself to focus on what he'd learned tonight. While he hadn't come any closer to finding out who was sending Stravos the letters about his daughter—and he'd shopped more today than in the past year of his life— he still felt like the day wasn't a total bust.

Meeting Stravos had been an interesting experience, but unfortunately had only left him with more questions than answers—the biggest, of course, being why was Sapphira afraid of him? And better still, why did Huck feel the pressing urge to protect her from him? He wished he could deny the feeling, wished that he could will it away—whatever problem existed between them was none of his business and wasn't his mission to fix.

Unfortunately, he couldn't shake the sensation that despite her wealth and privilege, Sapphira was like the proverbial bird in a gilded cage. Why else did she continue to live on the estate? Why hadn't she gone to work? He knew she had a degree. If she hadn't planned on using it, then why had she bothered with school at all? She'd graduated summa cum laude from Wellesley College—he'd seen the framed diploma in her living room. The wherewithal to manage that feat sure as hell didn't coincide with the unconcerned socialite shopoholic he'd seen in action today.

Put simply, none of it added up.

Secondly, watching the interaction between Sapphira and Ella had been particularly heartening. Sapphira obviously adored her former nanny—a helpful point he'd found in the file, along with Flanagan's "Good cook!" note scrawled into the margin. From what he'd been able to discern, Ella had been hired on within a week of the birth of the Stravoses' first child, Nicky, and had been with them ever since.

Though at twenty-six Sapphira was well past the needing-a-nanny phase, for whatever reason—in what he could only assume was either a rare act of kindness or sheer convenience—Stravos had kept her on. On salary? Who knew? But on the estate, certainly, and for Sapphira's sake.

Furthermore, though she hadn't told him as much, after visiting Ella's cottage, it was obvious despite the newer fixtures and appliances in Sapphira's house that hers was merely a replica of her nanny's. Odd that, Huck thought. With her resources she could have hired a premier architect and built any sort of house her imagination could have dreamed up. Instead, she'd opted for a carbon copy of her nanny's home. That was very telling, Huck decided. It told him that she was closer to her father's hired help than she was to her own family.

Frankly, though his mother had never been a nanny, she'd had clients develop a similar affection for her. To the extent of Sapphira and Ella? No. His mother had never been that accessible, had always refused to live on-site and had insisted that she maintain her own residence.

Because of him, Huck was sure.

When she came home at the end of the day, he'd never had to share her with anyone. Other than his grandmother, of course, but he'd never minded. They'd been close, Huck realized now, swallowing. He should probably thank her for that.

And he'd really never missed having a father, which made his sudden inescapable quest to find out the man's identity all the more strange. It didn't make any sense and yet he knew he'd never be able to rest until he *knew*. Had Huck wondered about him in the past? Certainly. And now that he had the time to focus some attention to the matter, he desperately wanted to know who the man was. He didn't want to *know* him, per se, and sure as hell didn't want to meet him. He just wanted the bastard's name and a face to put with it. He passed a hand over his jaw.

And he wished he didn't want that, because it felt like a betrayal to the mother who had loved and raised him so thoroughly.

At long last, Huck finally heard the shower stop and breathed a monumental sigh of relief. Why? Who knew? She was still dewy soft, wet and naked, those mocha curls smoothed away from her face and hanging down her back, beads of moisture clinging to her lashes…and other more intimate places. Another wave of heat washed over his throbbing loins.

Though the door to the guest bedroom was shut, he imagined being able to smell her soap, something clean and fruity with an orange-blossom finish. Imagined walking up behind her, filling his hands with her breasts and nestling his dick against the sweet warm *V* of her ripe bottom. Mercy, how he loved her ass. Biting her neck and feeling her quake against him, feel her sigh, weaken and tremble for him. Feel her arch into—

A knock sounded at his door, jerking him out of the fantasy. He shifted guiltily, and put the file he'd been looking at awkwardly over his lap. "Yes?"

Looking just as warm, wet and sexy as he'd imagined—complete with the sweet citrus scent—Sapphira poked her head into the room, careful to keep the rest of her body out in the hall. He could make out the top of a worn chenille robe and inwardly winced when he realized she was probably completely naked beneath the garment. Impossibly, more blood pooled in the fiery pit of his loins. "I just wanted to make sure that you found everything." She gestured toward his en suite bath. "Towels, soap and the like."

He nodded, wishing he could breathe. "I'm going to make one more sweep of the perimeter, check the locks and all before I shower and hit the sack."

Her eyes widened a bit and she nervously cleared her throat. "You're going to c-come into my room?"

Huck studied her and felt a slow smile spread across his lips. "Yeah. Does that bother you?"

He could only think of one reason it could and it absolutely tickled the hell out of him. Evidently he wasn't the only person battling an unwanted attraction. Now, *that* was an interesting turn of events—potentially disastrous, of course—but interesting all the same, Huck thought, irrationally pleased. How had he missed it? he wondered now as he watched her slightly anxious face, observed the dilated pupils, the way she worried that lush bottom lip. Classic signs of sexual interest, and he typically credited himself with a keen sense of insight…yet he'd missed them.

Probably because he'd been so worried about masking his own galling attraction, he decided, letting this new discovery inflate his ego right along with his miserably aching penis.

She moistened her lips and lifted her chin. "Not at all," she said. "I just wondered if you were going to do it from the outside."

"I can," he offered, smiling, his gaze tangling pointedly with hers. "If that makes you more comfortable."

She smirked. "That's okay. I'm comfortable in my own house, thank you."

"You should probably put on some clothes before I come in there," he suggested helpfully. "You wouldn't want me to get the wrong impression." *Or the right one,* Huck added silently, thoroughly enjoying himself at her expense.

She clutched the top of her robe, making sure the lapels were completely shut. She looked sexy as hell and strangely vulnerable in that moment. "Well, you're wrong about so much I can easily see you leaping to the wrong conclusion. I'm a light sleeper, so be quiet when you come in. Good night, Huckleberry."

"Not by a long shot," he said, chuckling softly.

But he had to admit it had just gotten better.

EFFECTIVELY SHUT DOWN from doing any in-the-trenches work, Sapphira spent the majority of the next day and afternoon working on the computer. Anytime she caught Huck looking over her shoulder—or anywhere in her direction, for that matter—she pulled up fashion Web sites and the occasional celebrity blog. She made sure to do a lot of loud sighing and tried to look bored out of her skull.

Frankly, she was neither.

The truth of the matter was that she liked her little house, and the last eleven days of being the world's biggest pain in the ass had been quite taxing. In short, she'd been exhausted and staying home was the perfect cure.

Furthermore, she'd been communicating with several people in her office, as well as managed to get a quick instant message to Carmen to let her know that she'd make the appointment tomorrow if it killed her. How was she going to handle that with Huck? Sapphira wasn't altogether sure at this point. But she would manage. She always did.

Last night when she'd been pretending to be asleep when he'd slipped into her room to make sure her locks were secure—as though she couldn't have handled that herself—she'd decided against bombarding him with a list of places to go. Sorting through a list of fabricated, frivolous errands generated to annoy him would not endear him to her. Better that she simply wait until the opportune moment and let him know that she had a doctor's appointment tomorrow morning.

She'd also managed to get a few e-mails to and from Cindy and, much to her pleasure and relief, last night's mentoring session had gone well. Reverend Alton had asked about her continued absence, but Cindy had smoothed things over, assuring him that Sapphira hadn't abandoned the project, but had merely been out of touch for the past couple of weeks.

Naturally, Cindy had been more interested in her first night with Huck than talking Belle Charities, but Sapphira had managed to mostly avoid the topic of her hunky bodyguard by citing her lack of privacy and limited time. Had they been on the phone, her friend would have no doubt detected the sheer unadulterated lust in her voice, the very tone she hoped with all her heart didn't come across to Mr. Ego. The look he'd given her last night when she'd slipped up and mentioned him coming into her room, had been absolutely mortifying.

He knew.

And she could, quite simply, kick herself.

She'd managed to pull off acting like a superficial prima donna for the past eleven days, then had dropped the ball on something like that? Irritation churned in her humiliated gut. If there were any way to kick her own ass, she'd do it.

She hadn't lied when she'd told him she was a light

sleeper, however, for the majority of the night sleep had completely eluded her and what few winks she'd managed to achieve had been fitful and punctuated with erotic dreams of him. The bastard-son-of-a-bitch-asshole, she silently added just to amuse herself.

Now, *that* had been a first.

Sapphira had never had a so-called wet dream before. Oh, she'd once dreamed of kissing Johnny Depp, but that was only after watching that pirate movie of his half a dozen times. No, this wasn't anything like that at all. Frankly, she'd almost bet a *real* kiss by the *real* Johnny Depp would pale in comparison to the *mere dream* she'd had of Huck.

Honestly, she didn't know whether or not he'd peeked into her room earlier in the day and therefore knew the layout of her suite, but the man didn't even have to let his eyes adjust to the darkness. He'd walked unerringly to all three windows in her room, systematically checking the locks, then had moved into her bathroom. Knowing he would do this, she'd purposely put all sorts of feminine products—nail polish and remover, astringent, lotion, a box of tampons, her birth control pills—in the windowsill just to trip him up.

He hadn't disturbed a single thing.

Then the wretch had had the nerve to come stand at the foot of her bed long enough to make her want to howl and had laughed softly, muttered a "Nice try, princess," then had quietly left her room to return to his across the hall. And that wasn't far enough.

By then, though, it had been too late. Her quarters had

been contaminated with his potent sex-appeal cooties and she'd turned into a miserable, aching wreck who'd wished she'd thought to bring some air freshener into her room to eliminate that wonderfully masculine smell.

His scent.

No doubt that lingering aroma had played a serious factor in her inescapable dream. Hot, hard body, supple muscles, smooth skin, that skillful mouth feasting upon her breasts, over her belly and ultimately between her legs. It had been the strangest—*most real*—thing. She'd literally *felt* him there to the point that she'd woken up in the middle of climax, her body dewy and quaking, and ultimately aching for him. Then, because she was a moron, she'd tried to fall asleep again immediately afterward so that she might recapture the magic and continue the dream.

She didn't, of course, but had to admit the human mind was a seriously powerful thing.

Her gaze slid across the room to where Huck sat, tapping away on his own computer. Other than a couple of trips to the bathroom, he'd been right there with her all day. Pinging her with his presence. Making her miserable. Her muddled belly gave a little flutter and a wash of heat engulfed her sex, causing her feminine muscles to clench. She forcibly squelched a whimper.

He looked up at her. "Is something wrong?"

"No, why?" she asked innocently.

"You made a noise."

"It's a silent scream of boredom."

He chuckled and shook his head. "Give it up. You're not bored."

She gaped at him. "How the hell would you know?"

"You've been too busy to be bored."

Sapphira closed her own laptop and stared at him. "Are you on crack?" she asked, feigning incredulity. "I haven't been busy. I've been surfing the Internet, filling my head with important celebrity gossip and fashion tips. Did you know that purple is supposed to be the new black this fall?"

"No, I didn't," he replied amiably. "And I can honestly say that I don't give a damn." He paused. "But you have not been bored. In fact, if I didn't know any better, I'd say you've been happy."

She felt a flush of heat climb her neck and decided that she'd better convince him that it was anger. "Happy? *Happy?* I've been your prisoner here all day. I've listened to you insult my dog, whine about my lack of proper snacks—like I'm supposed to know what sort of chips you prefer—and listen to you breathe all day long."

He chuckled and arched a brow. "You don't like listening to me breathe?" he asked. "Would you prefer the alternative?"

"No," she snapped. "I'd just prefer that you do your breathing somewhere else. Like Portugal," she added sweetly.

He paused, and a frightening flash of unreadable emotion lit up that keen hawklike gaze. She didn't know what imaginary line she'd crossed, but was suddenly aware that she'd gone too far. "Funny," he finally said. "I didn't get the impression you wanted me somewhere else last night."

Mortified, Sapphira sprang up. "Of, for the love of God. I saw the look on your smug face last night, hot-shot, and I've got news for you. I think you're laboring under the mistaken impression that I like you." She crossed her arms over her chest. "I don't."

Still smiling—oh, how she ached to wipe that self-satisfied look off his face—he merely shrugged. "You don't have to like me to want me."

She felt the floor shift beneath her feet and almost staggered from embarrassment. "W-want you?" she breathed, feigning outrage. "Have you lost your mind?"

"Nope. And I haven't lost my hearing, either."

She blinked, confused, though a hollow sense of dread had filled her stomach and spread to the point she couldn't feel her fingertips. "I'm sorry?"

"I heard you, Sapphira," he said knowingly. "Last night."

"I'm afraid I don't follow." A sneaking suspicion had taken hold, but it was too horrible—too mortifying—to contemplate.

"You called my name. Come to think of it, it was more of moan," he added, thoughtfully stroking his jaw. "I thought you needed help."

Her legs no longer able to support her, Sapphira sagged onto the nearest chair. He'd heard her sex dream, the one in which he'd had the starring, orgasm-inducing role? Dear God, where was a good hole when you needed one? She'd been embarrassed before. She'd walked out of a restroom with toilet paper stuck to her shoe, and she'd once done a combo sneeze/fart in an

elevator full of college-football players, but nothing—
nothing—compared to this. "You, er…" She cleared
her throat. "You came into my r-room again?"

"No," he said. He rubbed a hand over the back of his
neck, looking pleased but just a bit uncomfortable.
Probably wishing he hadn't let his ego loosen his
tongue. "I figured out what was going on before it ever
got to that point."

A small comfort, she thought hollowly as humilia-
tion saturated every pore in her body and manifested
itself in a full-body blush.

He'd heard her.

If anything this embarrassing had ever happened to
her before, her mind had blocked it from her memory.
She wished her bloody amazing mind would teleport
her to Portugal.

For the first time in her life, she didn't know what to
say. Somehow a "That's nice" seemed just a little too
inane. Rather than respond, Sapphira stood and started
to leave the room.

Huck suddenly rose out of the chair and stopped her
with the sheer force of his size. She almost landed
against his chest, and was actually angry when she
didn't. How screwed up was that? That she still wanted
to touch him—feel him, even accidentally—after this.

She felt his finger at her chin and he gently tilted her
face up to look into his. A shiver worked its way through
her and she felt herself gravitate toward him. "I'm sorry.
I shouldn't have told you."

He was right, dammit! He shouldn't have! Any sort

of gentleman would have kept his friggin' mouth shut. But was he a gentleman? No. Of course not. He was a badass former Ranger with wounded keen grey eyes, a fresh scar and a limp that begged more questions than she knew he'd ever answer. He was hard and annoying and arrogant. And funny and sexy and smart. He was… He was…

…going to kiss her, Sapphira realized a nanosecond before that beautiful mouth found hers. The very one she'd been dreaming about, fantasizing over.

He tasted like dill-pickle chips, ginger ale and something dark and thrillingly wicked. *Like sin,* she realized as her body melted against his. Her knees grew weak and her legs wobbled, forcing her even closer to him. Heat moved through her limbs and settled hotly in her sex, triggering a deep throb in her womb. She sighed, savoring the feel of him against her body. Her soft to his hard, strong hands framing her face, sliding into her hair and kneading her scalp.

Heaven.

A hum of masculine pleasure reverberated over her tongue and she ate it greedily, could feel the fire she'd been trying to contain blazing out of control throughout her body. And God, how she loved the way he felt. She'd touched men before, of course, but this one…

This one felt like warmed marble, living granite. Girl candy, Sapphira thought dimly as she felt his muscles bunch and bulge beneath her greedy palms. He was hot and hard—all of him—and she could feel him, like a fever, in every cell in her body. She wrapped her arms around his waist, then slid her hands over his back. Taut muscle, the vulnerable indentation of his spine, wide shoulders. He was like a drug and she was already hopelessly addicted.

It was madness, total insanity, and yet she couldn't seem to help herself. Couldn't get enough of him. She sucked his tongue into her mouth, slid it along hers in a particular dance that mimicked another more intimate act. His lips were firm, but full and moving over hers with an intensity that told her she wasn't the only one experiencing an inconvenient attraction—he wanted her, too.

The mere idea made her panties wet and she ached to rub against him, to put that hard ridge of arousal currently nudging her belly deep into the very heart of her. Instead, she scrambled closer and deepened the kiss. His big body vibrated with a need she recognized and answered with a moan of sheer madness. She felt his hands slide down her back, over her rump and he squeezed, setting off fireworks of heat in her sex. Warmth rushed to her core, coating her folds. Her nipples tingled and pearled and every press of his body against hers was a sheer delight of sensation.

Huck moaned into her mouth once more, suckled her tongue. "You drive me crazy, you know that?"

Now he wanted to talk? Mr. Brooding and Silent? Sapphira ignored him and pushed her hands back into his hair. She loved the way he felt beneath her palms, that delicate place behind his ear. So soft, she thought dimly. He nudged her belly again. *And so hard.*

She whimpered, began to tug the shirt from his waistband. She wanted to feel his skin, taste it, sample every inch of him. His smell, that wonderfully masculine fragrance, swirled around her senses. He slid his big hand up along her side, making a slow but determined journey toward her breast. She squirmed, trying to put the aching orb into his palm faster.

Almost… Almost…

Huck suddenly stilled and when he drew back, he looked every bit as flushed and feverish as she felt. Those gorgeous grey eyes had turned a deep gunmetal shade.

"Phone," he said, his voice oddly rusty. But he was quickly all business again. He swore and removed the cell from the holder at his waist. "Finn," he answered. His gaze suddenly cleared, sharpened and zeroed in on hers with unerring accuracy. "Another letter? When did it arrive? Okay. I'll be right there."

She smiled sadly, irritated on too many levels to properly count. One, another letter ensured that she'd continue to be an at-home prisoner, and two—she inwardly sighed—there was nothing like a little stalker to ruin a perfectly good kiss…which undoubtedly would have turned into perfectly *perfect* sex.

7

USING A PAIR of plastic gloves to keep from damaging
any potential evidence, Huck carefully inspected the
letter that lay on the foyer table, where the afternoon
mail had been deposited. Stravos wasn't there, but had
been informed of the letter's presence and had given instructions to turn it over to Huck.

After comparing it to the other two letters, he decided
this was definitely from the same person. Same style.
Local postmark. One simple sentence—*Sapphira's in
harm's way!*—and cut with pinking shears. An interesting choice, but readily available at any local sewing
center or craft store. He'd need to check it for prints, but
instinctively knew he wouldn't find any. He went over
the envelope once more, then shook it out to make sure
that he hadn't missed anything.

Beside him, Sapphira swore. "I wish to hell I understood this," she said, pushing her hair away from her
face. It was the first time she'd shown any real emotion
regarding the threat and he had a sneaking suspicion that
if she hadn't been so rattled over their recent kiss, she
wouldn't have slipped up. As it was, now he only won-

dered why she'd been hiding her concern to start with. Had she finally realized that this was more than an inconvenience?

"Does it mean anything to you?" he asked.

"Yes," she said, expelling an exasperated breath. Her green eyes snapped with irritation. "It means that I'm stuck here—" the *with you* was implied but unspoken "—for the foreseeable future, unable to go about my normal business. Dammit, I have things to do." Her back was ramrod straight, and her lush body—the one he'd been holding only moments ago—vibrated with impotent rage, pent-up anger and frustration.

That was an awful lot of emotion for thwarted shopping, Huck thought, studying her thoughtfully. He paused, a little alarm bell going off. Something didn't add up here. Granted, he'd spent only a little over twenty-four hours with her, but between her seemingly relieved-to-be-at-home morning—despite what she'd said, he didn't buy it—and this sudden outburst of emotion right now, he knew her better than that.

How did he know? Years of training, keen observation and an overall ability to judge character. For reasons he couldn't begin to fathom, she was determined to make him—and everyone else at Ranger Security— think that the only thing bothering her about these letters was the cramp it put in her style. Maybe so…but *what* style exactly?

Because he sure as hell no longer believed it was all about the shopping.

Nobody her age got that torn up over a missed pedicure or trip to the mall.

Seemingly aware that she'd shown too much, Sapphira made a visible effort to appear less concerned. "So…what now?"

Huck shrugged. "More of the same, I'm afraid. I'll send the letter over to Ranger Security and let them take a look at it, see if maybe they find something on here that I'm missing."

Her rigid shoulders sagged with a weary sigh. "This situation could go on indefinitely, couldn't it?"

"It could," he conceded, inclining his head. "But I don't think it will. The odds are whoever is doing this will slip up and when they do, we'll catch them. Until then, the only thing that we can do—and will do," he added pointedly, "is keep you safe."

She adjusted a single bloom from the arrangement on the table. "Here's the thing," she said. She looked up and those green eyes tangled with his. "I don't feel like I'm in danger. I should be afraid and, call me stupid, but…I'm not."

That was probably the most honest thing the woman had said to him since he'd met her, Huck thought, glad that they seemed to be making a bit of headway. "Why aren't you afraid?"

"Because these letters aren't really threatening." She gestured to the photocopies. "They don't imply bodily injury or death or anything else for that matter. They're more like warnings. The only thing that makes them a threat is what they *don't* say. It's what's left unsaid—the vagueness of them—that can't be ignored." Her lips twisted. "That's why my father hired you. Because ignoring them would have implied that he didn't care about me."

From the resignedly bitter tone of her voice, it was obvious that she thought her father *didn't* care about her, and frankly, after meeting the man, he wasn't altogether certain that he didn't agree. Was that why she'd resisted her security detail? Huck wondered. Because her father had only hired them to avoid the implication that he didn't care about her? Out of obligation instead of genuine concern? It was possible, he supposed, but it still didn't precisely fit.

His gaze slid over her once more, lingering over that lush mouth. In fact, at the moment, the only thing he could say that truly fit in this entire situation was her body against his.

Kissing her had been a monumental lapse in judgment, but he sure as hell wasn't going to say that he regretted it, because he didn't. He probably should, knowing that he wasn't going to be able to keep his hands off her, but…

Last night when he'd heard her softly moaning his name, the low hums of pleasure, the quickened breath and, ultimately, the keening cry of release, it had taken every ounce of strength he possessed not to walk into her room and slide into bed with her. Instead, he'd stood outside her door, his body locked in an eternal hell of sexual misery, his dick hard and aching, loins ablaze, and had waited until he knew she was enjoying a dream-free sleep before going back into his own room.

At which point, he'd promptly taken matters into his own hands, so to speak. A poor substitute for sure, but all that had been at his disposal at the time.

In retrospect, humiliating her by telling her that he'd heard her during the dream probably hadn't been the best choice, but the woman was so damn provoking he hadn't been able to resist. Frankly, he didn't think he'd ever met a female who had the power to annoy him quite the way Sapphira did. Drizzling sarcasm from that acid tongue, barbed comments designed to prick his irritation. She was a pro, he had to admit.

But she also wanted him.

And having her revert to the old routine after he'd rocked her dreams to the point of orgasm was just too much to take. He'd snapped, said damn the consequences, knowing full well that he'd just flushed his new career down the toilet. But he hadn't been able to control himself. If she'd have kept that infernal mouth shut, he wouldn't have had to take her down a peg with the I-heard-you comment, then he wouldn't have felt like an ass when she'd become so wretchedly embarrassed, and then he wouldn't have had to kiss her to make it all better.

In short, it was all her fault.

She'd brought his kiss upon herself and by God, if he ultimately snapped and seduced her, she'd have no one to blame but the person she saw in the mirror every morning.

Ridiculous logic, he knew, and yet accepting blame for any of it was out of the question because he simply couldn't believe or admit that he'd done something so unforgivably stupid. First assignment for Ranger Security—his new job, the one that was going to help rebuild his busted life—and he'd flubbed it already by crossing the sexual line?

Had he lost his friggin' mind?

Evidently so, because looking at her now, the taste of her still fresh on his lips, the feel of her lush womanly body melding with his, Huck could honestly say he'd do it again in a heartbeat.

Because he'd never had a kiss literally rattle him to the soles of his feet.

Huck had stolen his first kiss in second grade, had made his first sexual conquest with an older girl in eighth and had never had a problem attracting the opposite sex. By high school he'd honed his skills and had charmed the pants off any girl he wanted—time permitting, of course, because by that point he'd been working full-time—and had pretty much kept to that formula. If he wanted milk, he went to the grocery store. A steak? The local butcher. Sex? The nearest bar. It had always been that easy.

Because he'd been raised in a house with women who'd drilled respect into his marrow, Huck never took advantage, never made any promises and never walked away leaving a woman feeling used. That wasn't his style.

In short, he wasn't inexperienced and yet nothing could have prepared him for the utter circuit-blowing meltdown he'd encountered when his mouth had touched Sapphira's. It was almost as if his chemical makeup had undergone a change, an override of some sort.

She was soft and womanly, had tasted like peach

preserves and hot tea, and something else. Something indefinable and exclusively hers that had made him want to devour her, feed at her mouth until he got his fill—and instinctively knew he'd never get it—and then come back for more.

Until his cell had vibrated, the world had simply fallen away, existing only in that moment. Every sense had been heightened. *The feel of her hair sliding over the back of his hands, the smooth and delicate feel of her neck beneath his hands, her breasts against his chest, her small hands sliding over his jaw.*

Something about the sincerity in that gesture had made his throat tight and, because he'd mastered the art of self-preservation, he knew better than to wonder why.

Huck would like to think that he would have had the wherewithal to stop things from progressing be-yond a kiss, but if it hadn't been for the interruption, he feared the two of them would be tangled up in her bed right now.

If they'd even made it to the bed, which seemed doubtful.

The mere idea made his dick stir in his jeans, instinc-tively straining toward her.

In a moment they would go back to her cottage—just the two of them—and thanks to his "house arrest" mandate, they'd be stuck there together—*alone*—for the rest of the evening and, because of this newest threat, for the immediate future.

Funny, Huck thought as the Irony Fairy sprinkled her *ha-ha!* dust all over him. He'd put Sapphira in lockdown to preserve his own sanity and now he feared that very remedy would end up being what drove him insane.

"YOU'VE GOT TO COME over here," Sapphira hissed into the phone, peering around the corner to make sure Huck was still in the living room. "Bring an overnight bag and plan on staying. Indefinitely."

Cindy chuckled knowingly. "That bad, eh? What's happened? Ooo! Has he kissed you?"

Sapphira gaped at the phone. What? Was the woman psychic? "Can you just come over here, please?" she asked, purposely avoiding the questions—all of them.

"Sorry, can't," Cindy trilled cheerfully. "I've already got plans."

"Record *Dancing With the Stars,* dammit. This is important."

"So you've kissed him," Cindy said, sounding pleased. Sapphira could just imagine her friend's sly smile. "And from the plaintive desperation I hear in your voice, it was good. So good that you need a buffer, in the form of me?" She heard Cindy's hand smack against the table. "Oh, this just gets better and better."

"I don't need a buffer," Sapphira said, cowering from an imaginary bolt of lightning. "I need a friend. You're my friend, dammit. You're supposed to be here in my hour of need."

She chuckled softly. "Oh, I expect Major Finn could take care of you in your hour of need."

"*Cindy.*"

"Call Ella," her friend suggested. "She'll come over."

"Ella's at her book club meeting tonight." Besides, she couldn't ask her. Granted, she'd always been able to tell the older woman most anything, but somehow asking Ella to give up the comfort of her own bed and spend the night to keep her from sleeping with Huck was a little too much. A trifle over the edge.

Meanwhile, dinner was finished and there was nothing else to do. She'd tried reading a book. After reading the same passage a dozen times without retaining a single word, she'd given up. Watching TV? Ordinarily she enjoyed parking herself in front of the television with a plate of cookies and a cold diet drink—because, you know, having a regular soda would just be overkill and, despite evidence to the contrary, she didn't completely lack willpower—but she suspected that Huck's TV tastes and hers wouldn't mesh.

Besides, how could she think about anything but that kiss—and the resulting heat it had wrought in her body—with him in the room?

She couldn't.

Which was why she'd called Cindy and asked for her help. Sorry friend, Sapphira thought. "I can't believe you're doing this to me," she said. "The next time you have a crisis you're on your own."

Cindy's laugh came over the line. "Now, see, there's the difference between me and you. If I had a hot guy in my house and he'd kissed me, I wouldn't think it was a *crisis,* and, I hate to break it to you, sweetheart, but *you'd* be the last person I'd call."

Too true, Sapphira knew, smothering her own chuckle. Still, what Cindy would do wasn't helping her. Cindy wasn't a prisoner in her own house. Cindy wasn't the one being threatened. Cindy wasn't the one stuck here with a gorgeous man who made her thighs quake and her nipples tingle. Cindy wasn't the one who had to keep from embarrassing herself and she certainly wasn't the one who had to resist him.

No, that lucky person was her. And it bit.

Big-time.

"Sapphira?" Huck called.

"Dammit," she whispered. "I've got to go. He's bellowing."

"You make him sound like a caveman," Cindy said, laughing softly.

"He is," Sapphira said grimly. And it was no small part of the reason she found him so incredibly sexy. Who would have thought "caveman" would trip her trigger?

Struggling to pull the shredded threads of her composure around her, Sapphira disconnected the call and walked back into the living room. "Did you want something?"

Huck frowned at her. "What were you doing?"

"I was on the phone."

"With who? You're flushed."

Perversely, more blood rushed up her neck into her face. "My boyfriend," she said, seizing upon the fabricated excuse. "He makes me hot," she added, just to needle him.

Huck's deep chuckle rumbled up his throat and those silvery eyes crinkled at the corners. "You don't have a boyfriend."

She felt her brows knit. "How would you know?"

"Because it's not in the file."

"The file?" she asked, alarmed. "You have a file on me?"

"Sure."

"Let me see it," she said, opening her palm in a hand-it-over gesture he completely ignored.

"Sorry, that's privileged information."

Sapphira felt her mouth sag open. "Privileged information?" she parroted, stunned. Her hand dropped back to her side. "It's about me, but I can't see it?"

He winced regretfully, though she could tell he was enjoying himself, the wretch. "That's what makes it *privileged*." He said the word as though she were a half-wit, which made her want to smash things and scream.

"I know what privileged means, you arrogant jack-ass," she snapped. "What I want to know is why is it privileged *from me?*"

"Arrogant jackass." Seemingly proud of the insult, he smiled at her and the soles of her feet tingled. "That's a new one."

"I have more. The file?" she prodded.

Huck sighed. "There is no file. I made it up."

"What?"

"I made it up."

"Why on earth would you do that?" she asked, her voice climbing. God, the man infuriated her. She didn't know when any man had ever managed to get under her skin quite the way that Huck did.

He lifted one muscled shoulder into the semblance of a shrug and smiled unrepentantly. "I was bored. Pissing you off entertains me."

Pissing her off entertained him? *Entertained him?* She'd been a bundle of sexually miserable nerves for the past two days—magnified to near torture as a result of that brain-frying bone-melting near-orgasmic kiss— and he was bored? Needed entertaining? She mentally added a few more choice names to the ones she'd called him—some of them anatomically impossible— and concentrated on not springing across the room like a spider monkey on crack and pummeling the hell out of him.

"If you didn't have a file, then how did you know that I didn't have a boyfriend?" she asked instead. What? Was she wearing a sign? *No significant other here, last date two months ago? Doomed to remain single?*

Huck studied her thoughtfully before responding and that intense scrutiny left her feeling raw and exposed. "I can just tell."

"Because I haven't had a date? Because no one has called? How do you know my boyfriend isn't out of town, or even out of the country for that matter?"

He sighed heavily. "You don't have a boyfriend."

"But you can't know that," she insisted. She didn't know why this was so important, but it was.

He paused and quirked a brow. "Do you have a boyfriend?"

"No, but that's beside the point."

Those silvery eyes widened and a bark of laughter erupted from his throat. He straightened in his chair and passed a hand over his face, evidently trying to erase a smile. "There's a point to all of this?"

"The point is that I could have a boyfriend if I wanted one," she said through gritted teeth. "And you can't know if I have one or not."

"But I was right. So I did know."

"No, you *suspected,* but you didn't *know*. There's a difference." She smiled sweetly at him. "It's subtle, so you probably missed it."

Huck stood, unfolding all six and a half feet of him from her recliner, and sidled toward her. She got a mental image of a hawk circling above her and a giddy thrill tripped down her spine. But there was nothing subtle about the way his gaze traveled up her legs, lingered over her breasts and mouth, and then ultimately slammed into hers. The breath thinned in her lungs, her heart pounded so hard she could hear it thundering in her ears to the point that she was almost deaf. Though everything in her screamed *"Retreat!"* and *"Run, fool, run!"* Sapphira said goodbye to self-preservation and stood her ground. She tilted her chin, refusing to give up an inch of space.

"Let me tell you what I didn't miss," he said, his voice low and gravelly and just a bit dangerous. "I didn't miss the way you kissed me a little while ago. I didn't miss the little moans of pleasure I ate from your mouth and I sure as hell didn't miss the way that you want me."

He inched closer, seemingly daring her to argue. "I know you don't have a boyfriend because if you did, you wouldn't have kissed me, or even wanted to for that matter." A little smile played over his increasingly closer mouth. "Despite evidence to the contrary, you aren't nearly as shallow as you've been pretending to be."

"I haven't been—"

He interrupted her lie. "Why have you been pretending? Who knows? It's a mystery for another time. But if I had my guess, you were on the phone with a friend just now—probably Cindy—trying to arrange an interruption because you know as well as I do that if something doesn't give soon, we'll be in bed faster than you can say 'charge it.'"

Sapphira blinked, equally impressed and terrified that he'd pegged her so damn thoroughly.

"Shut up, Huck," she whispered, looping her arms around his neck as the inevitability of this moment crashed around her, bringing anticipation, joy, fear and breathlessness. "Nobody likes a know-it-all."

8

MIRACLE OF MIRACLES, Huck thought dimly as his mouth latched hungrily onto hers—she wasn't arguing. Didn't try to deny it or even put up the token protest.

Instead, true to form, she'd made a smart-ass comment, then prevented him from uttering one in return by striking with a preemptive kiss.

Only a moron would complain and, while he had to admit he couldn't claim full cognitive reasoning at the moment—because all the blood had rushed to another part of his anatomy—he was not, and had never been, a moron.

At the moment, he was simply on fire. And hungry. For her.

The kiss, urgent and unplanned, had snapped something inside of him, had set off a reaction he should have realized was merely waiting for the opportunity to present itself.

Given the way her body was pressed tightly to his, the urgency in her kiss, the slide of her small hands over his body, that moment was now.

In the darkest corner of his mind, Huck realized that he should stop this, that sleeping with her would surely be the end of his professional career with Ranger Security and an end to something else, less definable, but there all the same. He knew this and yet he also knew that walking away from her—actually *stopping*—was out of the question.

Physically, he couldn't do it.

That alone set off a warning bell loud enough to rattle his insides, but didn't so much as make him flinch away from her.

For reasons he couldn't explain and couldn't reason, Sapphira Stravos, the mouthiest little rich girl he'd ever met, had the power to turn him inside out…and perversely, he looked forward to the destruction.

More specifically, he looked forward to coming apart inside of her.

With that thought in mind, Huck picked her up and started toward her bedroom.

"Put me down," she said, startled. "I'm too heavy."

Huck carefully set her on the bed and followed her down, kissing the side of her neck and nipping at her earlobe. "Obviously that's not true."

Her eyes warmed with pleasure. "But what about your knee?"

Huck chuckled softly, systematically undoing the buttons that marched down her shirt. *Smooth skin, swell of plump breasts…* "Darlin', that injury is well south of the part of my body I'm going to need for this."

She laughed, more of a wicked hum in her throat. "That's not what I meant."

He knew what she meant, but it didn't matter. He slid

a finger over the lacy edge of her bra—one he recognized from their recent shopping spree—then bent and ran his tongue along the tempting swell, causing her breath to catch in her throat.

He'd never heard anything in his life as erotic as that one telling sound.

"Pretty," he murmured huskily.

Sapphira's fingers tunneled into his hair and he felt her roll more firmly toward him, aligning the hardest part of him with the softest part of her. "Bet you wish you'd carried it for me now, don't you?"

He popped the front clasp and had the pleasure of watching her lovely breasts come free of their flimsy restraints. "No," he said. "But I'm going to like taking if off of you." Then he bent his head and pulled one achingly perfect dusky nipple into his mouth.

She arched against him and another mewling noise issued from her throat. The sound swirled around his senses as he circled the bud with his tongue and pulled deep, savoring the taste of her in his mouth. Musky, fruity, the taste of woman. Oh, God, he could devour her. He cupped the other breast, rolled her nipple between his thumb and forefinger and felt her press her hips against his, silently begging for what he desperately wanted to give her. Release and redemption, the disease and the cure.

She tugged at his shirt and he broke away from her long enough to let her drag it over his head. She tossed it aside, then whimpered as his belly touched hers—skin to skin.

He quaked.

The sensation was so foreign it took a second to process, but before he could fully assimilate the emotional implication, Sapphira arched up and shrugged out of her shirt and bra, then her fingers found the button of his jeans and whatever profound thought that had been about to surface swiftly fled.

He inhaled sharply as her fingers slipped beneath his waistband. Impossibly, he hardened even further and his dick throbbed with every beat of his heart. The whine of his zipper punctuated the silence and he felt his jeans sag away as her hand suddenly wrapped around him. A groan tore from his throat and he bent once again and fed at her breasts, suckling hard as she worked the slippery skin against her palm.

Desperate to feel even more of her, Huck slid a hand down her sweet belly and carefully unsnapped her pants. Less than a minute later, even her panties—pretty, sheer and purple, which matched the bra—lay on the floor with the rest of their clothing.

Fully naked. At last.

He smoothed his hand over her hip, tracing the full womanly curve, then over her lush rump, the very one he'd been lusting after for what felt like years. He gave a gentle knead and she reciprocated by slipping her thumb over the engorged head of his penis. He jerked against her and growled softly because it felt so damn good.

But not as good as she would taste, he knew.

Huck worked his way down her abdomen, kissing every other rib, licking a path around her belly button, then parted her soft brown curls and fastened his mouth upon the very heart of her. Her taste bathed his tongue in a flavor so wonderful he groaned from the pleasure.

Sapphira fisted her hands into the bedspread and bucked beneath him, a keening cry smothering in her throat.

He smiled against her and suckled more, paying close attention to that kernel of sensation nestled high in her folds. He worked his tongue, laved and lapped, feeding at her as though he were a starving man and she his last feast. He sipped up her womanly juices, bathed his index finger in them and then tucked it deep inside.

Her feminine muscles tightened around him, offering a prelude to what would come next, those soft, wet walls closing around him as he pushed inside of her. The mere thought brought him almost to climax.

"Huck," she said, her voice broken and raw with desire. "Please. I can't— I need—"

He knew what she needed. He needed it, too.

Desperately.

What he also needed was a condom and to his immediate horror he realized he didn't have one. He swore. "Sapphira?"

Her hands slid over his shoulders. "Yeah?"

"I, uh… I don't have a condom."

She leaned forward and nipped at his neck. "Bedside drawer," she said. *"Hurry."*

Relieved beyond measure, Huck didn't allow himself to think about the fact that she kept the protection readily available—for other men, obviously, which was intolerable—but rather decided to focus on the positive, like the fact that he was about to be inside of her, burying himself to the hilt in her softness, feeling her tighten around his aching dick, her breasts against his chest and her nails biting into his ass.

He quickly opened the package, withdrew the protection and swiftly, hand shaking, rolled it into place. The instant he was finished, she pushed him onto his back and straddled him, her hot weepy folds settling over him. He instinctively nudged, his head pushing up against her clit.

She whimpered, winced with pleasure and glided over him, coating him with her juices. "Sapphira," he growled warningly. If she didn't take the control she wanted soon, he was going to steal it back from her. Of course, that was assuming he'd ever had any control to start with and that, he knew, was doubtful.

She bent forward and laved his nipple with her tongue, slid her greedy hands over his chest, mapping him wonderingly. She frowned when she reached the pink puckered scar on his side, carefully skimming her fingertips over it before pressing a delicate kiss against the wound, as though she could make it all better now.

Before he could form the first cynical thought, she raised her hips and settled down on top of him, absorbing every inch of him deep inside her. He watched the breath leak out of her lungs, her chest deflate with pleasure, as she seated herself firmly over him.

Huck set his jaw so hard he thought he heard his teeth crack. Sapphira, in that moment, was the most beautiful thing he'd ever seen. Beautiful lips swollen from his kisses, caramel curls tumbling over her shoulders and teasing the tops of her full, ripe breasts. Sweet belly, the flare of her curvy hips, that patch of dewy curls seated against him, and her ass—

Sweet heaven, the woman had an ass that simply would not quit. Lush and heart-shaped, perfect for his hands, he thought as he slid them around and shaped her to him.

She arched up, then slowly sank back down, clamping around him—holding on as though she couldn't let him go, couldn't feel enough. The mere idea made his chest swell with some sort of caveman pride and he leaned forward and pulled a nipple into his mouth, suckling hard, flattening the crown of her breast against the roof of his mouth.

She cried out, tensed and rode him harder. Up and down, up and down, tightening and tightening, refusing to let him go. He kneaded her rump and thrust hard against her, could feel his aching balls drawing up in preparation for climax.

Her first, Huck thought, biting the inside of his cheek as the orgasm gathered force.

He bucked beneath her again, suckled the other breast and ground his hips against hers.

Ah…the magic combination, he thought as her entire body went rigid with release and her mouth opened in a soundless scream. He watched her breasts jiggle and heave as the climax washed over her, felt her fist around him over and over, her neck go all but boneless, barely able to support the weight of her own head, much less the rest of her body as she collapsed on top of him.

No worries, Huck thought as he rolled her over onto her belly, dragged her hips—that delectable ass—into position, then pushed into her from behind. She wasn't going to need any more of her own strength.

THE ORGASM HAD BEEN so intense Sapphira's vision had blackened around the edges and hadn't returned to proper focus before Huck had taken control and, impossibly, another climax hovered just out of reach. She could feel it building deep inside of her with every powerful thrust. His big hands were spread in an almost territorial fashion over her ass, kneading, stroking, with every push of him deep within her.

Though she knew it was physically impossible, Sapphira could *feel* him in every cell of her body. He'd infected her, she thought as his scent coiled around her, drugging her, making her boneless and rigid, sated and yet energized, and with every delicious draw and drag between their joined bodies—with every brush of his balls against her aching flesh—she wanted more.

More of this.

More of him.

More of them.

She sank her teeth into her bottom lip, whimpered and pushed hard against him, desperate to take every enormously glorious inch of him. Her breasts bounced back and forth on her chest, absorbing the force of his thrusts. Her nipples tingled with the remembered warmth of his mouth.

Harder, deeper and harder still.

"I...love...your...ass," Huck said, punctuating each growling word with a reverent squeeze.

Since the lamentable size of her ass had always been a sore spot with her, he couldn't have uttered a single compliment that would have pleased her more. A rush of feminine pride washed over her, bringing a smile to her lips.

Another bright flash of tingly warmth ignited in her womb, the fuse to another bone-melting climax sizzling along until the orgasm detonated in a fiery ball of sensation that ripped the breath from her lungs and made every muscle tense in awe as it surged through her. Colored lights spotted her vision, marking the occasion with a blazing display behind her closed lids.

Huck leaned forward, nipped at her shoulder, then she felt him stiffen behind her and a long bellowing groan worthy of a caveman tore from his throat. He held her tight and pushed hard, angling deep as he pulsed into her, jerking from the force of release.

Desperate to see him—to *watch* him come into her—Sapphira turned her head and gazed over her shoulder at Huck. Lips peeled back over his teeth, shoulders and forearms absolutely locked in a sinewy display that would forever be emblazoned in her brain, Lucas Finn epitomized the word *virile* in that moment. In fact, she could say beyond a shadow of a doubt that she'd never seen a man so beautiful in his masculinity. The thought sent another tingle rippling through her sex and she squeezed around him once more.

Huck's gaze tangled with hers, smoky and sated

and loaded with male satisfaction, and something shifted around her heart. Something dangerous and ill conceived and just plain stupid because it had no place here.

But before she could completely panic, he slid his hands over her bottom once more, then carefully—reluctantly, she could tell—pulled away from her. She immediately missed his warmth, the feel of those big wonderful hands on her body.

With the help of a tissue he'd grabbed from her nightstand, he made quick work of the condom, then drew back the covers and settled her in beside him. Despite the protection in the bedside drawer, she'd never had a man in her bed before.

It was…nice, Sapphira decided. Because it was Huck.

The moment begged for conversation, for a compliment or at the very least a thank-you. He'd just given her the very best sex—and very best orgasm—of her life and yet…Sapphira couldn't think of a single thing to say.

She waited, hoping he'd contribute something.

He didn't. He doodled his fingers on her upper arm, drew lazy circles and seemed to be completely content. He sighed into her hair. She concentrated on the heavy rise and fall of his chest beneath her ear, the delicious feel of her smooth leg slung over his hairier one. On anything but what lay unspoken between them.

But…how the hell was that possible after what they'd just shared? How could he simply lie there and not say anything? Because he couldn't think of anything positive? she wondered, becoming ridiculously paranoid.

What? If he couldn't say anything nice, then he wasn't going to say anything at all? Was that his game?

Fine, Sapphira thought. Besides, this was probably the only way she'd ever have the last word. Pasting a smile on her face, she snuggled in closer to him and sighed as though all was right in her world. And curiously, because she was with him, she could almost believe it.

"Huck?"

"Hmm?"

"I need to tell you something."

"Sure."

"I've got an appointment with the gynecologist in the morning."

9

Feeling like the proverbial only rooster in the henhouse, Huck shifted miserably in the squeaky leather chair in Sapphira's gynecologist's office and pretended not to be uncomfortable—*pretended* being the operative word.

Truth be told, he felt so damn twitchy it was a miracle his skin hadn't started flaking off.

When Sapphira had announced last night—immediately following the best sex he'd ever had in his life, because she was evil—that she needed to go to the gynecologist today, Huck had known one single blinding moment of panic. Visions of VD and antibiotics had flashed in his postorgasm fuzzy brain, but then sanity had returned in the form of her laughter, and he'd relaxed.

In the first place, they'd used protection, and in the second place, he instinctively knew she was healthy. After all, he thought, feeling a wicked grin slid over his lips, she'd *tasted* fine.

She'd rattled off some nonsense about a bad Pap smear—whatever the hell that was—and how the test had needed to be redone. He shouldn't worry—she was fine, she'd assured him. It was merely a precaution, and while they were out, could they please drop by her favorite coffee shop and that was all.

She promised.

Considering that she hadn't asked to go anywhere in the past couple of days and she'd chosen a time when, admittedly, he would have told her she could fly to the moon if she'd had a rocket available, Huck had simply toyed with her breast, sighed heavily—because he was doomed—and said yes.

Then, because he knew this job was going to come to the same disastrous end as his last career, he'd said to hell with it all and spent the entire night in her bed, punctuating the wee hours with the best sleep he'd had in years and the best sex…*ever*.

Honestly, he'd known the attraction—the sheer force of her appeal—had exceeded anything in his extensive experience, but nothing—*nothing*—could have prepared him for the absolute annihilation of his self-control and resulting response.

He hadn't just wanted her—he'd *had* to have her.

Impossibly, even sitting here in this wretched doctor's office while feminine atrocities were being conducted behind closed doors, he could feel the heat writhing in his loins, creeping up his dick.

He should have been satisfied. Shouldn't have the friggin' strength. And yet, if she walked out that door right now, he knew beyond a shadow of a doubt that he could take her.

Gratifyingly, he also knew—not simply *suspected,* as she was so keen on pointing out last night—that she wanted him, too, that she'd let him. Thankfully, whatever mad fever had corrupted his own blood, brain or what have you, had infected hers as well. No brag, just fact, but Huck knew when a woman wanted him. A lingering look, quickened breath, a shallow sigh. Those were nice. But nothing compared to being the object of her affection.

She had to taste, touch, sample…everything.

She was fearless and tireless and completely uninhibited. He hadn't had to coax a single response from her, hadn't had to jump through the usual seduction hoops. She'd wanted him and she'd had him—repeatedly—and this morning, when there could have been an awkward moment between them, Sapphira's bright green eyes had warmed with pleasure and, a sleepy smile still on her lips, she'd pressed a kiss against his cheek and then rolled out of bed, completely naked, citing a necessary visit.

Minutes later they'd been sharing coffee and slathering jam over bagels. It had been…easy, Huck realized now, and disturbingly domestic.

At some point he knew that he'd have to discuss the ramifications of a sexual relationship with her—after all, this was the woman who'd already asked for a replacement once—but at the moment he wanted nothing more than to simply enjoy spending some time with her. And no doubt that would lead to having more sex with her, and since he didn't seem physically capable of keeping his hands off her, this was probably the most realistic plan to try to put into action.

His cell vibrated at his waist once again—he'd already fielded another call this morning from his P.I., who'd yet to turn up anything on his father—temporarily giving him a reason to do something other than stare at the poster of the female anatomy adhered to the wall. "Finn."

"We've been over the letter you couriered yesterday afternoon and it's clean," Payne said.

Dammit, Huck thought, unsurprised. Were they ever going to get a break? "I figured as much," he told him, passing a hand over his face.

"How's the house arrest going?"

"Better than expected," Huck said, flushing with a guilty smile. "We're out right now actually. She had a doctor's appointment."

"Don't tell me she's back at the gynecologist?"

Huck stilled, a memory niggling just out of reach in the back of his mind. "Yes," he said cautiously. "What? You've been here before?"

"Just last week," Payne said. "For a yearly pelvic exam, according to her. But it's funny because I got the impression she'd been there a lot recently. All the nurses were on a first-name basis with her and one of them made the comment 'It's not long now.' If I didn't know any better, I would have thought that she was pregnant."

The female-anatomy poster he'd been staring at spun at an odd angle and his mouth went bone dry. "P-pregnant?" Huck asked, coughing on the word. Surely not. He'd know, right? Wouldn't he have been able to tell? Wouldn't her breasts have been tender? Her belly a little full?

Pregnant?

"She's not," Payne said. "I point-blank asked her and she said no. Frankly, I've always been good at picking up on a lie and my gut told me she was telling the truth." He paused. "But I do think it's a little odd that she's back there already. What reason did she give?"

"That she'd had a bad Pap smear and it needed to be redone. I'm, uh… I'm not familiar with the test and I—"

"Hold on," Payne said, cutting him off. Huck heard him call out to someone else—his wife, maybe?—then ask a series of muffled questions. "Okay, Emma says that it's possible that the original test got botched, but…I don't know. I don't trust her. My internal alarm is going off here."

His, too, Huck thought, staring at the door where Sapphira had gone inside. He'd insisted on sitting in the hall rather than in the waiting room. How was he supposed to protect her if he didn't know where the hell she was? he'd argued, much to her annoyance.

"Let me ask you something, Payne," Huck said speculatively. "Did you wait in the lobby or go back with her?"

"She wouldn't let me go back with her, but I refused to wait in the lobby. We compromised by letting me guard her examining-room door."

"Right. That's what I'm doing as well. Did you go into the room and inspect it first?"

"I tried," Payne said. "She wouldn't have it."

Huck hummed under his breath. He was beginning

to see a pattern here. He'd wanted to scope things out as well and she'd acted as though he were a total moron for even suggesting it. And since this was her territory, so to speak, he'd relented.

Clearly that had been a mistake.

Because what had even become more transparent was that she was hiding something.

Again.

Huck smothered a long-suffering sigh and told Payne he'd keep him informed.

"Do," Payne said. "I'm getting a weird vibe."

His conscience twinging with the uncomfortable knowledge that he'd just slept with his first assignment and that it was a shitty damn way to thank the men who'd taken a chance on him, Huck muttered a "Sure thing" and disconnected.

Then, after less than a moment's hesitation, he stood up and made his way to the door to the room where Sapphira had disappeared more than twenty minutes ago. The doctor, a short Indian man with a warm smile, had gone inside while Huck had been on the phone with Payne. He leaned in and listened intently.

A strange, watery *thump-thump-thump* sounded, followed by an unmistakable "Aw. Isn't that wonderful?"

Not Sapphira's voice, Huck thought, frowning. A nurse? He didn't think so. A nurse had ushered Sapphira in, but hadn't lingered. She'd exited shortly thereafter and not another single soul, with the exception of the doctor, had gone into that room. He'd be willing to bet his life on it.

"A nice strong heartbeat," a heavily accented voice confirmed. The slide of wheels across the floor, then, "Let's check you and see where you are this week."

A strong heartbeat? Check her? Whose heartbeat? And check who? Dammit, he needed to be in that room. None of this made any sense and a horrible sensation had taken root in his gut. He strongly suspected someone in that room was pregnant, and if it wasn't Sapphira, then just who the hell was it? Was that what she'd been hiding?

"Can I help you?"

Huck started and turned around to find another nurse, this one scowling and unfriendly, staring at him. He upped the charm wattage, hoping to soften her, but didn't believe for an instant it would work. "No thanks, I'm just listening."

"If you were allowed to listen, then you would have been invited into the room." She lifted her chin. "I'm afraid I'm going to have to ask you to leave."

Oh, shit. Since it hadn't worked, Huck abandoned any pretense of charm and blanked his face of any emotion. "And I'm afraid I'm going to have to refuse. I'm Sapphira Stravos's security detail and I'm not going anywhere."

Her nostrils flared as she inhaled an incensed breath. "Then kindly return to your seat. It's impolite to eavesdrop," she pointed out, directing a pudgy finger at an uncomfortable chair.

Though he didn't particularly care for her imperious gesture or the criticism, Huck decided it would be better to heed the woman than cause a loud scene. While he'd like nothing better than to charge into the room and find out exactly what was going on—and were he still a Ranger, that's the precise strategy he would have employed—he knew his current line of work wanted more finesse.

It was a mystery, Huck decided, one he had every intention of solving.

And when he'd put all the pieces together, he planned to share them with Sapphira…and dare her to take them apart.

"CARMEN, YOU'RE fifty percent effaced and dilated a centimeter." Dr. Borgu shrugged. "You could deliver any time now. As we discussed last week, it's normal to have a little spotting and mild contractions after you've been checked, so don't worry about that. If, however, your contractions become regular and are five minutes or less apart, or your water breaks, then go directly to the hospital."

Smiling, Carmen nodded. Seemingly satisfied, the doctor shook her hand and left the room. Sapphira quickly moved to the door to make sure that Huck wasn't going to try to steal a peek into the room. Honestly, she wouldn't put it past him. He'd tried every way in the world to accompany her into the exam—which wouldn't have been a good idea even if she'd really been having another Pap smear—and she'd had to heave many an exasperated sigh to restrict his presence to the hallway.

Carmen's dark gaze found Sapphira's. "You're going to come to the hospital, right? You'll be there?"

"I promise," Sapphira told her, offering a reassuring smile. No matter what it took, she wouldn't let her down.

Honestly, looking at Carmen—at the grace and strength she'd shown at seventeen while dealing with an unplanned pregnancy and impending motherhood—Sapphira knew her own problems, annoying though they were, paled drastically in comparison. Carmen had repeatedly thanked her for her support, had reiterated her appreciation over and over, but what the younger girl didn't understand was that you couldn't put a price tag on what Carmen had shown *her*.

She'd been so brave, so strong, had matured with an inherent efficiency only impending motherhood could have brought about. She looked at Carmen, listened to her baby's heartbeat and knew had her own baby survived, she would have been strong enough to do those things as well. Was it hard, when she missed her own unborn child with every beat of her heart? Yes. But it was worth it.

That, Sapphira thought as she watched Carmen rub a hand over her swollen belly, was utterly priceless.

"So have you thought anymore about what we talked about?" Sapphira asked her.

Carmen hesitated. "You mean the job?"

"And school," Sapphira added. She'd talked to her cohorts at Belle Charities and they'd unanimously decided to put Carmen on staff as a permanent mentor for unwed mothers. Unlike the rest of them, she'd be a paid employee, with benefits. They'd also agreed that a job without an education wasn't going to suffice.

Carmen had the brains, the drive and the ability to do so much more and, ultimately, to teach other women like her how to accomplish the same things. While the other mentors would offer support and advice, Carmen's first-hand experience would validate her in ways the rest of them could never imagine.

In short, her story would make her a credible mentor for their cause, and investing in her and her education was a sound financial decision.

"I appreciate the job offer, Sapphira, you know I do," she said, her chin tilting at a familiar proud angle. "But the scholarship is too much. I can't accept it. Working is one thing. You know I'm not afraid to work—"

Too true, Sapphira knew. Despite the hell it had wrought on her back, Carmen had held on to her job at a local bookstore and had continued to go to school.

"—but I won't take that sort of handout. It's too much."

"Carmen, it's a hand *up*, not a hand *out*. There's a difference."

She started to shake her head. "I don't think—"

"Carmen, please. You need this," Sapphira said, taking her hand. She grinned. "And your baby is going to need it, too."

Carmen smiled weakly, looked away and shook her head, clearly on the verge of relenting. "It's low to play the baby card, you know that, don't you?"

"I'll do whatever I have to do to get you to say yes," Sapphira needled. "Little Esmerelda is going to need an educated mother."

Carmen's dark eyes widened. "Esmerelda? I'm not

naming this baby Esmerelda," she said, wrinkling her nose in distaste.

"Then what *are* you naming this baby?" It was a game they'd played since the beginning and a carefully guarded secret as far as Carmen was concerned. While it would have driven her insane, Carmen had even refused to know the sex of the baby. "Ten fingers? Ten toes? Everything is where it's supposed to be? Then that's all I want to know."

And she'd meant it, insisting that the baby's gender be a surprise.

"You know I'm not telling you until it's born," Carmen said. She glanced at her watch and winced. "I've got to hurry. My shift starts in less than an hour."

Sapphira felt her brow wrinkle. "Are you sure you need to go to work?"

"I'm sure I need the money," Carmen said, ever practical. She gathered her purse, hugged Sapphira tightly and thanked her again for attending the appointment with her. "You keep that cell on and fully charged," she instructed. "I'd hate to have to storm the gates of your hoity-toity estate." She chuckled softly. "How's the new bodyguard working out?"

Sapphira had told her about Huck yesterday in their brief instant-message conversation. The mere thought of him made the tops of her thighs burn, and remembered heat throbbed in her sex. "He's a caveman," she said. "But he's not that bad."

Carmen stilled and she stared at her long enough to make her want to squirm. "You *like* this one," she breathed, seemingly stunned.

What the hell? Sapphira thought as panic punched her pulse into overdrive. Had she become that pitifully transparent? Sapphira cleared her throat and tried to appear nonchalant. "He's nice enough, I suppose. If you like that sort of thing."

Carmen's eyes twinkled. "He's a nice caveman?"

She chuckled and looked away. "A misnomer, I know, but…yeah." And he was, Sapphira realized, in his own sexy, boorish way.

"And you like him." She said it with an implied ooh-la-la and rocked back on her very pregnant heels.

"Stop that," Sapphira admonished. "You'll fall over."

Carmen frowned. "Hey, I'm *not* that big."

No, but she was that counterweighted, Sapphira thought. She bit her tongue and kept the comment to herself. "Of course not." She hugged her again. "I should go. Give me a couple of minutes to get Sir Pain in the Ass out of the hall before you come out, okay?"

The younger girl chuckled. "Sir Pain in the Ass? How does he feel about that nickname?"

"I wouldn't know," Sapphira quipped in a near whisper. "Because he doesn't know about it." She winked and quickly made her way out into the hall, where Huck sat.

That silvery hawkish gaze did a slow once-over that started at the tips of her toes and ended when his gaze found hers. Humor, heat and something else, something thrillingly dangerous and deliberately guarded, hovered there, making her breath hitch in her throat and a single dart of alarm land in her heart.

Something had changed, Sapphira realized. She didn't know what—couldn't even begin to imagine—but the status quo had shifted sometime between the minute she walked into that room and the instant she'd walked out of it.

She hesitated, the barest betrayal of her sudden unease, then plastered a smile on her face and hoped that he wouldn't notice. Futile, she knew. The man didn't miss a friggin' thing. But… "I'm ready," she said and started down the hall.

Huck stood. "I'm not."

Sapphira drew up short and turned around. A funny taste developed in her mouth. She labeled the flavor panic. "Sorry?"

"I've got to pee. Where's the bathroom?"

Her eyes widened, and every second they spent in the hall put her that much closer to discovery. "You couldn't go while I was in there?" she asked, pointing at the examining room.

He smiled. "I was guarding you," Huck said. "I couldn't leave my post. Where's the bathroom?"

Sapphira looked desperately up and down the hall, could feel her blood pressure heading toward stroke level. Huck *could not* see Carmen. Everything she'd worked for—everything she'd accomplished—would all be at risk. Her involvement with Carmen would go into the report to her father. He'd start asking questions and poking around, discover the extent of Belle Charities and her involvement in it and…and…

She'd be finished.

And all the girls and families who depended on her would be left in the lurch.

She couldn't let that happen.

Sapphira hurried over and grabbed his arm and in loud, carrying tones said, "This is a gynecologist's office, Huck. They don't have a men's bathroom. Come on," she said, tugging him toward the exit. "You can pee in the bushes outside. That ought to appeal to you."

Huck dug in his heels. "I don't want to pee in the bushes outside. I want to pee in here. If I didn't know any better, I'd think you have something to hide in here."

Her throat parched. Any second now Carmen was going to walk out that door and the jig would be up. Furthermore, for whatever reason, she knew he was stalling. She'd spent the past three days with him and the man had an iron bladder. A few steps to the parking lot wasn't going to cause him any physical injury. He was being bullheaded and belligerent and had evidently caught the scent of a mystery, one she *could not* let him solve.

For the first time since this all started, Sapphira wished she could confide in him, wished with every fiber of her being that she could share her real life with him, not the one she'd been forced—and was still being forced by her father—to portray.

She hesitated, looked up at him and longed to unburden her soul. She wanted to entrust her secrets and unburden her heart, to make him more than a lover, but a friend as well. She instinctively knew he'd be a good one, loyal and true, honest and frank. And in the deepest part of her soul, particularly after last night, intuition told her he could be so much more.

More than she dared to hope for.

Because, ultimately, he worked for her father. And that cast more than one fly in the ointment—it put every other unsavory insect in there as well.

The thought, however depressing, braced her. He had to guard her, right? Well, he couldn't do that if she left. Unhappily reverting to her prima donna roll, Sapphira turned and walked down the hall. "I'll wait in the car."

He hesitated—*one, two, three*—then muttered a curse and hurriedly caught up with her.

Back ramrod straight, Sapphira inwardly wilted with relief. Geez God, but how much longer could she keep this up?

Better still, how the hell was she going to keep herself from falling head over heels in love with him?

10

"ARE YOU SURE you can behave yourself in here?" Huck asked as he held the door open to her favorite coffee shop. He had grim memories of the last time they'd darkened this door and didn't want a repeat performance of her there-isn't-enough-foam-on-my-latte rant.

Sapphira had the grace to blush, and a droll smile rolled around her lips. "I'll be fine," she said. "And when I'm not, I tip well. Just ask Mark."

"Who's Mark?"

She nodded toward the twenty-something hippie boy behind the counter. "That's Mark."

The boy smiled when he saw her. "Where's Trixie?"

"She's at home today," Sapphira told him.

Mark inclined his head. "The regular?" At her nod, the boy's gaze swung to him. "What for you, sir?"

"Coffee. Black."

Mark looked momentarily confused, but eventually smiled, revealing a set of dimples on each cheek. "Kickin' it old school, eh, chief?"

Old school? Huck thought with a mild frown. Evidently catching his look, Sapphira chuckled softly under her breath and those unusual green eyes sparkled with humor. She snagged a chair and settled into it. "You're thirty-something, right?"

"I'm thir*ty*," he clarified, shooting Mark a glare. "Not thirty-something."

"Well, to him it doesn't make any difference." She waggled her brows significantly. "You're old."

"I'm not old," Huck insisted, needled. Hell, thirty wasn't old. Did he miss his twenties? Certainly. They were some of the best years of his life. But hell, he wasn't ready to shuffle out to the retirement home just yet. "It's not like I'm playing bingo and researching the best denture adhesive." He paused. "How old are you exactly?"

"What?" she asked dramatically. "You mean that isn't in the file?"

Actually, it was. Mark arrived with their drinks, then quickly moved away. "You're twenty-six, right?"

Sapphira swore, but there was no heat in the expletive. "Dammit, can't I have any secrets?"

Huck felt a chuckle break up in his throat and he inclined his head. His gaze tangled intently with hers. "Oh, I think you've got several."

Looking as if she wished she could gnaw off her tongue, she shifted and casually licked the foam from the top of her latte Mark had just handed her. Whether she meant it to be a sexual gesture or not, Huck couldn't help but react. After all, that hot tongue of hers had been licking *him* just last night. Heat coiled in his belly and spread into his loins, forcing him to shift.

"Me?" she joked. "You're the mystery man. You've got a file on me and I know absolutely nothing about you."

Huck poked his tongue in his cheek. "Carnal knowledge doesn't count?"

Her eyes twinkled and, clearing her throat, she reached into her purse and withdrew a small bottle of hand sanitizer. "You know what I mean."

Rattled her that much, had he? he thought, unreasonably pleased. "And the file is not *on you,* specifically," Huck felt compelled to point out. "It's about your case."

"Do you typically sleep with your cases?" she asked, throwing it right back at him.

Huck nodded. "Yes."

She blinked, stunned, and her mouth dropped open in evident shock. Strangely, she seemed to have lost the ability to speak. He patted himself on the back for that one and absently scratched his chest. "You're my first case," he explained, "and since I've slept with you, I guess I'd have to call it typical, wouldn't I?"

"I'm your first case? Seriously?"

"And probably my last with this firm." He winced, then smiled. "I'm going to need to go over the employee handbook, but I thinking sleeping with you was probably against the rules."

She snorted. "Then don't tell them. I'm certainly not going to, and I'd advise you to keep it out of the report you send my father."

He felt a half smile shape his lips. "You almost sound worried about me."

She cocked her head as though she was confiding something important. "Hey, you might be a son-of-a-bitch-asshole-bastard-unsufferable-boorish clod, but I'd hate to see you murdered."

He smiled. "You think your father would kill me?"

She made a moue of distaste. "Not in the literal sense."

"Sweetheart, better men have tried. I'm not afraid of your father."

A shadow moved over her gaze and she looked away, stared at passersby on the street through the plate-glass window. "That must be nice," she said. "He scares the hell out of me."

"What are you so afraid of?" he asked, surprised by how much he wanted to know. Not just to satisfy his curiosity or to help make sense of this case, but because he wanted to alleviate those fears. Fix them for her. Did he have the power to do that? Probably not. Should he want to do that? Hell no. But he couldn't seem to help himself. She brought out a protective streak in him, one that he would have never imagined he possessed. In fact, she had the uncanny ability to bring a lot of things out in him, things that made his gut clench and a fluttery warmth breeze through his chest. Things he didn't know how to explain or compartmentalize. He told himself that she made him crazy, that the phenomenally hot sexual attraction had skewed his perspective.

He told himself that and prayed like hell he'd eventually believe it.

Sapphira's lips twisted into a sad smile. "I don't want

to talk about my father," she said. "Here's a thought. Why don't we talk about yours."

He made a derisive snort and took another sip of his coffee. "That'd be a short conversation."

"Why?"

"Because I've never met the man." The admission shocked him, rattled him to the soles of his feet. What the fu— What in God's name had possessed him to say that? Why would he—

"I'd wondered," Sapphira said, seemingly unsurprised. He didn't detect a single inkling of pity—which would have set his teeth on edge and generally make him want to tear the room apart—just genuine interest. "When Ella asked about your family, you mentioned your mother and grandmother, but not your dad. You were too deliberate for it to have been an oversight."

And he obviously wasn't giving her enough credit, Huck thought, impressed that she'd noticed. "You don't miss much, do you?"

"It pays to pay attention."

Yes, but to what? Huck wondered. What had her attention? And more importantly, who had been in that room with her today? And why was that such a secret? He could ask her, of course, but in futility, he knew. If she'd wanted him to know what was going on, she would have told him already. Clearly he had some more poking around to do—a new investigation to launch— and instead of focusing on who was sending the letters, Huck thought his time would be better served concentrating on her.

He smothered a dark laugh. As if he could concentrate on anything else.

"So…you've never met your father. Does that mean you don't know who he is, or just aren't interested in making his acquaintance?"

"Tell you what," Huck said. "I'll answer you when you tell me why you're afraid of your father."

Sapphira merely smiled. "You're stuck on that, aren't you?"

"I want to help you."

Her gaze softened and she smiled sadly. "I wish you could."

"What makes you so sure that I can't?"

Another weary smile slid over her ripe mouth. "Stop being so nice to me," she said. "I don't know how to act."

He felt a laugh rumble from his chest. "Have I been that terrible?"

A wicked gleam lit her gaze and she chewed the corner of her lip. "You made up for it last night."

"If you're trying to flatter me by telling me that I'm good in bed then…go ahead," he finished magnanimously, releasing a pent-up breath. "I won't try to stop you."

Sapphira stared at him a moment, almost wonderingly, then chuckled. That warm, feminine laugh struck a chord deep inside him and settled intimately around his heart.

"I thought you said you needed to go to the bathroom," she reminded him.

He'd lied, but telling her that probably wasn't a good idea. Of course, neither was squandering a perfect opportunity, either, he thought as visions of her back against a wall, him pushing inside her suddenly filled his head. Ordinarily sex in a public place wasn't his thing—he preferred a little privacy—but he'd been itching to climb back into her body from the instant he'd left it last night, and now, sitting here with her, intrigued and consumed with the irrational need to save her, Huck didn't think he'd ever wanted a woman more. She drove him insane. Tore him up and pulled him inside out.

But he knew the second he had her—the second he settled into her heat—that he'd be fine. The madness— the sheer insanity of whatever was happening to him— would recede, and for the moment, he'd be able to breathe.

"I do have to go," Huck said, standing abruptly, thankful that he'd had the foresight to snag a few condoms from her bedside stash. He grabbed her arm and tugged her along with him. "And since you can't leave my sight, then you're just going to have to come with me."

"Into the men's room?"

"Don't be a sissy. Aside from the urinal, it's exactly the same."

He pushed open the door, then shut it and flipped the lock.

"Can't I just wait outside?" Sapphira said, shooting a distasteful look around the bathroom. No doubt she could feel the germs leaping onto her body, Huck thought, smothering a smile. For reasons he couldn't begin to fathom, he found her germiphobia adorable. "Ooh, Lord, I'm going to need an entire bottle of hand sanitizer after this."

Huck sidled closer to her, backing her up against the

door. "I take exception to that remark. You didn't mind my germs last night."

Gratifyingly, her gaze darkened to a mossy hue and she moistened her lips. "It's not your germs that I'm worried about."

Huck lifted her off the floor and pressed a no-holds-barred, I'm-going-to-fuck-you-senseless kiss against her lips. "Here," he said. "Let me see if I can distract you."

Then he rocked his hips against hers and smiled against her mouth as a little gasp of pleasure eddied from between her lips.

"You make me crazy, you know that?" he asked, feeling marginally better now that she was in his arms, kissing him as though she needed this as much as he did.

"And you talk too much," she said, wrapping her arms around his neck. "Focus, Huckleberry. *Focus.*"

THERE WAS NOTHING quite like having the undivided attention of Lucas Finn, Sapphira thought as his big warm hands shaped her rump and squeezed. And, oh, how that warmed her heart. He made a low growling noise in the back of his throat that absolutely made her go all gooey inside. She could feel herself melting, coming apart, getting needier and wetter with every slide of his tongue against hers, every greedy masculine sound echoing between their joined mouths.

Whatever he suspected—and she knew that he definitely realized something was going on—it didn't keep him from wanting her, didn't keep him from being able to deny the white-hot, uncontrollable attraction between them.

Had she ever been this mindless? Sapphira wondered. This desperate? Had she ever felt as if her skin was going to burn off her body if *his* lips didn't put out the blaze? Had she ever hungered for the taste of a man so much that her mouth actually watered?

There was a sweet spot just above his cheekbone, but not quite at his temple where his skin was so soft it made her eyes water and her chest yearn for unnamed things and terrifying emotions. Things like happily ever after and dark-haired children with mirrored gazes, sleeping late on rainy days and sharing dawn over a hot cup of coffee. Christmas morning and new family traditions. It made her long for a family of her own—desires she'd never truly plumbed until now. Because they'd been out of reach? Because she hadn't found the right partner? Why? Who knew? But there was no denying them now, no pretending that everything could just go back to the way it had been.

He'd changed her, Sapphira realized in an inconvenient moment of insight, as her pants gathered in a knot around one ankle and his fingers slipped her panties aside.

He rolled a condom into place and she felt him nudge her weeping folds, felt her breath leak out in a relieved sigh and realized just how far gone she really was.

She was about to have sex. In a public restroom. Germ heaven, billions of bacteria. She swallowed a hysterical laugh. And she didn't care. She didn't reach for her hand sanitizer—she reached for him.

Muscled shoulders bunched thrillingly beneath her hands as he lifted her hips and settled her on top of him. She felt herself stretching, welcoming, relishing every enormous inch of him. The door at her back, a big wall of hot hard man at her front, inside of her...

Sweet Lord.

Sensation bolted through her, energizing every cell in her body. She leaned forward and licked a path up the side of his neck, then nibbled on his earlobe. She'd found that little detonator last night and loved knowing that she could set him off as easily as he managed to ignite her flame.

Huck growled, much like the caveman she'd been calling him. "Sapphira," he said warningly as he pumped even harder into her.

She tightened around him, gasping with pleasure. "What?"

Another deep thrust, and another and another, swooping into her. Her hips banged against the door in a steady *thump-thump-thump* she dimly realized would probably draw some attention. She didn't care about that, either. "You're killing me," he said.

She smiled against his lips, sucked his bottom lip into her mouth. "Yeah, but you like it."

He chuckled softly. "You're awfully sure of yourself."

"Why wouldn't I be?" she asked, clamping around him once more and hearing a gratifying hiss—her proof, so to speak—slip out of his mouth. "You want me."

He laughed again. "I don't suppose it would do any good to deny it," he said, flexing into her once more, his hips rhythmically pistoning in and out of her, pushing her closer and closer to the edge of climax. Every thrust, every slide of him deep inside of her made her belly clench and her sex sing.

Sapphira rubbed her thumb behind his ear, cupped the back of his neck with her hand and drew him in for another kiss. "I know this is going to come as a surprise," she whispered. "But I want you, too."

She ate his laugh, savored the taste of his masculine smile on her lips. "I had my suspicions," he said. He slid his tongue down her neck, nipped her shoulder, causing a shudder to ripple through her and vibrate her belly. "But it's always nice to have those suspicions confirmed."

"What can I say? I aim to please."

"No," Huck teased. "You aim to annoy…but I happen to find that intensely sexy." He punctuated the statement with a deliberate shift of his hips that unerringly found her G-spot. Little lights danced behind her closed lids and she inhaled sharply.

"Was that supposed to be a compliment?"

"Ah," he sighed, chuckling knowingly. "There it is. Does it really matter?" He nudged deeper and quickened the thrusts, snatching her breath with each push of him against her.

"No," Sapphira admitted, smothering a string of curses as the world around her feet began to fall away. She bit her lip and held on, felt her body priming for release, readying for that unique moment when she'd die in his arms and he'd breathe life back into her with the aid of his kiss.

"Huck, I want— I need—"

"I know what you want," he said, his voice rough and sexy. "Tell me what you need."

He pushed high and aimed deep, nudging her womb, filling her so completely she didn't know where he ended and she began and she didn't care.

She just needed him.

Had to have him, right there between her legs, emptying her out and making her whole, wringing every bit of strength from her body. "You know I need you, dammit. I—"

"Say it," he growled. "Please."

Something in his voice shook her to her very soul— yearning, longing, desperation and despair, a hell she knew well, one she didn't want to be alone in, either. She clamped around him, hugged him tight to her body and put her lips next to his ear.

"I need you, Huck," she whispered, the admission broken and breathless, laying her bare, leaving her vulnerable.

A racking sigh emptied out of his chest and he bucked *hard* into her. The edge of climax he'd been pushing her toward suddenly loomed, bright and brilliant, and with one final thrust, she tumbled into that dazzling luminosity with a long keening cry of release, which he ate greedily.

One, two, three more plunging into her quivering, convulsing flesh and he stiffened, locked his knees and buried himself completely into her. He didn't move, just pulsed inside her. Those little throbs detonated further sparklers of pleasure, causing her to tighten around him. A pool of warmth gathered in the back of her womb—his seed in the end of the condom—and it belatedly occurred to her that he'd told her he didn't have any protection.

"Huck, where did you get that condom?"

"From your house. I thought it might come in handy," he said. He pressed a kiss to her forehead.

"For future reference, I'm on the Pill."

He smiled against her. "I know."

A weak chuckle broke loose in her throat and she waited for her pounding heart to return to its natural rhythm. "Don't tell me, that's in the file, too."

His lips slid into a wicked smile. "No. I saw them on your windowsill, remember? When you were trying to sabotage me?"

That felt like a lifetime ago, Sapphira thought. "Oh, yeah."

He sobered. "You want to tell me what's really going on? What really happened at the doctor's office this morning?"

Sapphira felt a balloon of dread pop in her chest. She'd known this was coming, had known he'd want some legitimate answers. "I want to tell you," she admitted.

He waited, then, "I'm sensing a but."

She rested her forehead against his and sighed. "But I can't. So don't ask, Huck, because I don't want to lie to you."

"So we're going to have to do it the hard way?"

She smiled sadly, wishing with all her heart that it wasn't so. "It's my MO, I'm afraid."

The wrong way, the hard way, they were pretty much interchangeable when it came to her, Sapphira decided.

Huck carefully withdrew and lowered her onto the floor. Her legs were rubbery and she immediately missed his heat. She felt his thumb slide over her chin and he tilted her head up. His gaze was warm and resigned. "I suspected as much," he said. "Just don't get pissed off at me when I uncover your secrets."

That was only fair, she decided. After all, he was only doing what he was being paid to do. Unfortunately, if he found her out then she'd have to label his modus operandi "seek and destroy."

Because she'd be ruined.

11

"ADMIT IT," SAPPHIRA cajoled. "She's growing on you."

Snuggled into the curve of his arm, the two of them huddled together watching old *Andy Griffith* reruns—common ground was a beautiful thing, he thought, thankful they'd found a program they both liked—Huck chewed the corner of his mouth to keep from smiling. "Who's growing on me?"

She certainly had, there was no denying that. And yesterday, after their impromptu sex in the bathroom at the coffee shop, he'd stopped trying to convince himself that what he was feeling was simply ordinary.

There was nothing average about the way she made him feel, the way his body reacted to hers.

But that wasn't what she was talking about and he knew it. His gaze slid to the dog, who'd curled up on his lap, and he squashed a grin. Pussy had taken a shine to him.

"Trixie," she said, reaching over to rub the little dog's ears. "You like her. Admit it."

"She'll make an excellent snack for the real dog I'm going to get," Huck said, much to Sapphira's outrage.

She shot him a look. "Real dog? Are you implying that she's not real?"

"She's a toy," Huck told her. "And, I gotta tell ya—" he winced regretfully "—she's not the sharpest knife in the drawer."

"Huck!"

"Sapphira, she can't even play fetch." It was true. He'd tried tossing a few of her toys around in an effort to bring out a little of the canine in her behavior and she'd batted the damn things across the floor, as though she were a cat. Clearly she had some sort of cross-species thing going on.

Sapphira's pert nose shot up into the air. "Fetch is overrated. She does lots of other cute things."

He had to admit that watching her chase her own tail—another feline trait—was pretty amusing. Huck patted the little animal's back and was rewarded with a delicate lick of his hand. "You can't help it if you're a bit dull, can you, Pussy?"

She gasped and punched him playfully on the upper arm. "Huck! I told you to stop calling her that." Her cheeks pinkened. "It's crass."

"Yeah...but you like it."

And he liked making her blush, which was why he kept using the nickname. Sapphira was gorgeous in any right, but something about watching that wash of color spread over her cheeks, that bashful smile slide over her mouth, made her even more beautiful. More compelling.

Furthermore...her? Bashful? When there wasn't an inhibited bone in her body when it came to making love? It was just another one of those complex contrasting facets of her personality that made her all the more interesting. He loved that about her. Huck inwardly grinned. Which probably made him as neurotic as she was.

After her heartbreakingly weary don't-make-me-lie-to-you comment yesterday, he'd refrained from asking any more questions. Instead, in between the time they'd spent in bed, in the shower, in the bathtub and on the couch, he'd started a bit of research on his own. Using the file Ranger Security had amassed on Sapphira's case and the daily reports of her comings and goings, Huck had noticed an interesting pattern.

In addition to the two doctor's appointments, at every single one of her so-called beauty treatments, her friend Cindy Ward had been present. He knew that girls tended to move around in packs—hell, you rarely saw one go to the bathroom alone—but something about that had struck Huck as odd. It was almost as if they were meeting. But why the secrecy? It didn't make any sense.

The only other place she'd gone besides the various retail outlets, spas and coffee shops had been Dr. Borgu's office and Belle Charities.

Initially, when he'd first begun on the case, Huck had written it off as a minor blip in the overall radar of her life. Lots of rich people had pet charities and organizations they liked to contribute to, more so usually to garner good press and rub elbows with the right people than out of a true giving spirit. Seeing that Sapphira had made a twenty-minute stop at their humble headquarters downtown hadn't set off bells.

But after looking at the rest of the time she'd been out, it was obvious that one little stop had been more telling than any other.

A quick search had revealed that Cindy Ward, the convenient and always available best friend, was also second-in-command at Belle Charities.

To his ultimate shock, he learned that Sapphira was the head honcho of the organization, and though he'd discovered they like to keep things very low-key, the foundation helped *a lot* of people. Most particularly, they worked in conjunction with a shelter downtown headed up by a Reverend Alton, and one of his key in-ititatives happened to be—surprise, surprise—a mentoring program for young, unwed mothers.

No doubt that attributed to her frequent visits to the doctor's office, he thought, impressed with her kindness. No doubt one of the girls she was mentoring was about to deliver. That also explained the fetal heartbeat he'd heard, the "almost there" comment Payne had remarked upon. And she gave more than her money, she gave up her time as well.

Clearly, Sapphira didn't want her father finding out about her involvement. Why? He couldn't begin to imagine. Couldn't wrap his mind around any possible reason Mathias Stravos would mind his daughter helping those less fortunate.

Ultimately, though, he didn't have to wrap his mind around it. Obviously he still didn't have all the facts, and more than likely wouldn't until she decided to share them with him.

Because the root of all mysteries could usually be solved by following the money trail, Huck had called Payne and asked if he could do a little poking around in Sapphira's finances. Frankly, while Huck could do a few crude searches from here, the kind of information he wanted called for a more finessed hand.

In short, Payne's extensive wealth could get him answers Huck didn't have a prayer of acquiring on his own.

Not only had Payne come through, but he'd managed it in record time. In less than an hour from the moment Huck had contacted him, Payne had returned his call and had given him the 411. Though she didn't actually "work" for Stravos industries, she was on a mind-bog-glingly ridiculous salary with the company and, here was the kicker, more than seventy-five percent of her income went into Belle Charities.

Was that the problem? Huck wondered. Would her father object to how she spent her unearned money? And if so, then why put her on salary? Why give her any money at all? His gaze slid to the diploma on the wall. Better still, why didn't she work?

None of it made any damn sense.

In fact, he wished he could say that the mystery sur-rounding her and her comings and goings was the only thing that seemed illogical, but frankly…there was nothing the least bit rational about the way she made him feel, either.

She made him stupid, Huck decided. Why else would he not seem to be overly concerned about the fact that he was going to be unemployed when he told Payne, McCann and Flanagan about his affair with her? That he would once again be a ship without a rudder? A free agent without a plan?

Sure, she'd suggested that he keep that little kernel of information to himself, but unfortunately, he wasn't wired that way. He'd made the call—he refused to label being with her a mistake—and he'd own it.

The end.

But would it go in any official report he filed with the company or with her father?

Hell no.

And that was more to protect her than him. Sapphira walked on pins and needles around her father under normal circumstances—he sure as hell wouldn't give her any other reason to be afraid of the coldhearted bastard.

Furthermore, ultimately, it wasn't any of her father's business.

Shaky ground, he knew, because he essentially worked for the man. Still… He'd been hired to protect Sapphira, and if keeping information from her father fell under that purview, then so be it.

His gaze drifted over the achingly smooth slope of her cheek, the shape of her beautiful mouth, and lingered around her eyes, and a swelling warmth spread throughout his chest. Sheer panic and an emotion so pure it hurt tangled around his heart, making his palms tingle and his breath thin.

The question was…who was going to protect him from her?

Because, whether he liked to admit it or not— whether he *wanted* to admit it or not—he'd unwittingly handed her the power to hurt him.

Lucas Finn had survived some of the most intense military training on earth, had jumped from airplanes directly into enemy fire, had battled other opposing soldiers and faced terrorists who relished the possibility of death.

But he'd never known genuine fear. Real, bone-chilling she-could-break-my-heart horror.

Until today.

Because, he'd realized, nothing was more terrifying than falling in love.

"WHAT DO YOU MEAN you're going to get a dog who will think Trixie is a nice snack?" Sapphira asked, taking the opportunity at a commercial break to go back to that little nugget of information.

For reasons she couldn't begin to explain, Huck had finally started answering some of her many questions this afternoon. Why? Only he knew, she supposed, but she wasn't going to linger over the question. The happy fact and important thing to keep in mind was that he was *finally* beginning to open up. The tidbit he'd shared yesterday about never meeting his father had been an accident, she was sure, because when she'd tried to plumb the topic further, he'd repeatedly changed the subject.

Today, however, or this morning more specifically,

after he'd taken that last phone call, he'd been more willing to share. He'd also looked at her as though he'd never truly seen her before and that narrow scrutiny had made her feel as though he could see through her, could peer into the deepest corner of her soul. She found the sensation equally reassuring and strange.

"I mean, once we find out who's threatening you and this case is over, I'm going to get a dog."

"Really? What kind?"

"A big one," Huck said, glaring at Trixie. "From the animal shelter."

"Big dogs aren't always good for apartment living," Sapphira pointed out. He'd mentioned that Ranger Security had provided a place downtown as part of his employment package.

Huck slid her a look and grinned, his smile the epitome of wicked. "You just want me to get a sissy dog to match yours."

"They don't have to match," Sapphira told him, though admittedly that would be cute. "I would just prefer that your dog not eat mine, that's all." It was the closest she'd come to alluding to the fact that she wanted things between them to continue after all of this mess was over.

Honestly, when Sapphira had started using her mock salary for charity work, she'd essentially accepted that she would be permanently indebted to her father. That she would have to hide her work in order to keep the money coming in and going out.

What she hadn't factored in at the time was how that indebtedness would essentially prevent her from ever truly breaking free of her overprotective yet mostly absent parent. How his approval and ability to control the purse strings would ultimately give him the power to orchestrate her life as he saw fit.

Until now it had never been a problem. She'd been content and happy. For the most part, he'd left her to her own devices and she'd come and gone as she pleased, periodically dated, but had never been serious about anyone. She'd been so focused on what she was doing that she'd never fully explored what she'd be giving up to keep up the status quo.

Sapphira looked into the future now, one that she longed to share with Huck, and saw a quagmire of problems and a landmine of obstacles to overcome.

Bottom line, Mathias Stravos would never approve of Lucas Finn. It wouldn't matter that he'd fought and served for his country, had been wounded as a result of that service—another tidbit he'd shared. She'd been intrigued by the new scars, the angry one, in particular, across his knee, and he'd finally told her about the training mission gone bad.

In one fell swoop, he'd lost his career.

The blink of an eye and life as he'd known it—his entire purpose—had changed. Then Ranger Security had given him a home and he'd squandered it on her, Sapphira thought, hoping with all her heart that he'd avoid the honorable thing and not tell them about their affair.

She knew better, of course. That's one of the things she'd grown to really respect about Huck. What you saw was what you got—no subterfuge, no games, all honesty all the time.

Even when you didn't necessarily want to hear it.

That took a rare kind of courage—character one didn't always find anymore. He was a rare breed, she decided, with a true sense of duty and honor and responsibility. Simply put, he was a good man, her Falcon. Yet another tidbit she'd gotten from him this morning—his military nickname. One that fit, she thought, her gaze caressing the lean slope of his cheek, those piercing gray eyes.

And she grimly suspected she'd fallen in love with him.

When had it happened? Probably the first instant she'd laid eyes on him. She'd known, hadn't she, that he was different? That he was special? Hell, her body had recognized it long before her heart and head had caught up. She'd been burning for him—in a constant state of longing—from the minute he'd walked into her living room and told her not to call him a son of a bitch, an asshole or a bastard.

She blushed, remembering that she'd called him worse.

But it didn't matter, because at the end of the day, despite the heartache she knew was going to inevitably come, she just wanted to be with him.

She wanted to kiss those masculine lips, taste that patch of skin behind the shell of his ear. Trace each rib with her fingers and learn his body in Braille. She wanted to claim every part for her own, burrow beneath his skin and make him feel all the wonderful things she was feeling. She wanted to see into his head and share his thoughts. Heal his pains and help him over the hurdle of losing his passion.

God, how she'd heard that in his voice. When he'd talked about floating along in the sky, that first rush of adrenaline he got from jumping out of a plane, the way his stomach would lurch when he pulled the ripcord and the sense of pride on every successful landing...

He hadn't simply enjoyed what he'd done—he'd been in love with it.

Huck caught her staring at him and smiled. "What are you thinking about?" he asked cautiously.

"You and your Falcon days," she said, considering him thoughtfully. "I would have loved to see you jump out of an airplane. You're an arrogant badass now." She rolled her eyes. "I'll bet you would have been damn hard to live with back then."

"Arrogant badass?" he parroted, feigning outrage. "I'm not arrogant, Sapphira. I'm *good*. There's a difference. It's subtle," he reminded her. "So you might have missed it."

Throwing her words back at her, was he, the wretch? "It's nice to see that your self-esteem wasn't damaged in the fall," she said drolly.

"No, the only thing that got wounded, aside from my body, was my pride." He swore softly and looked away. "Stupid mistake."

She felt a frown furrow her brow. "What happened?"

The light dimmed from his eyes and his gaze grew shuttered. "Doesn't matter, does it? I can't fly anymore."

Intuition told her it did matter, and because she was nosy she couldn't let it go. "You don't make stupid mistakes. Something must have happened."

She waited and he rewarded her patience with a long sigh. "I got lost in thought, let my mind wander for an instant too long. By the time I realized that I'd missed the drop zone, it was too late. I was already in the trees."

Lost in thought? About what? It had to have been something important. She threaded her fingers through his and studied the strength in each knuckle, committed every line to memory. "What were you thinking about?"

His gaze finally found hers once more and a humor-less grin slid over that sensual mouth, one that somehow managed to break her heart. "My father," he finally said, a bark of ironic laughter tearing out of his throat. "It's funny. I hadn't thought about the man in years. It seemed like a betrayal to my mother, you know. She'd worked so hard, so tirelessly, to make a home for me, to make sure that I never lacked for anything, and so I never really…missed him." A ghost of a smile played over his lips. "She wouldn't allow it." He paused. "But a fellow trooper had lost his father that week and I started thinking about mine. Did I have any brothers and sisters out there? If so, what were they like? Had I passed them on the street? Had I passed *him* on the street? What was he like? Was he even still alive? I've even hired a P.I.," he added. He swallowed. "One thought led to another and the next thing I knew, I was screwed."

Her heart ached and she snuggled closer to him, trying to absorb his pain. "Oh, Huck, I'm so sorry."

"I've got nobody to blame but myself," he said, suddenly sobering.

And he did, Sapphira knew. "We all make mistakes,

Huck," she said. "And sometimes the hardest person to forgive is ourself."

She knew. She'd gone through a brief period where she'd blamed herself for losing her baby. She had to have done something wrong, otherwise her baby would have survived. Ella had told her otherwise, of course, had explained that miscarriage was nature's way, but it had still been hard.

She'd also blamed herself for Nicky's death. She hadn't noticed that he'd been spiraling out of control, she hadn't taken every phone call, she hadn't connected the dots. Her fault, she'd thought. If she'd only done something—anything—different, then her brother would be alive. She shared as much with Huck, then shrugged. "Ultimately, I realized that hindsight is twenty-twenty and that I couldn't have changed the outcome. Am I sorry that I didn't pay more attention? That I missed his cries for help?" She nodded. "Every day. But there's nothing I can do to change things, and the guilt finally got too heavy. Ella convinced me to put it down and move on."

"She's a wise woman," Huck said, nodding thoughtfully. "Do you know why your brother took his own life?"

Sapphira shook her head. "My father thinks he pushed Nicky too hard and, while I won't lie and say that didn't contribute, I think he just…got sick of living. He'd always been a bit troubled. Dad had reamed him out for making a poor investment, his girlfriend had just broken up with him. He hated the business, had always dreamed of pursuing an art career."

Something sharpened in his gaze and he glanced around her living room. "Are those paintings his?" Huck asked.

She nodded, emotion welling in her throat. "Yeah," she sighed. "He was very talented."

"I'm sorry, Sapphira. That must have been tough."

She leaned her head against his chest. "It was. But it gets easier. We were close and I miss him, but time has a way of making things that were unbearable…bearable. You learn to endure."

He pressed a kiss on the top of her head. "Those are wise words, sweetheart. Thank you for sharing that with me," he said, that smooth baritone achingly earnest, silently begging for more.

She longed to bare her soul to him so much in that instant that it hurt, that keeping it in felt like a festering sore in her belly. *Do it,* a little voice prodded. *Tell him about Carmen. Tell him about your baby. Tell him about Belle Charities. Tell him who you really are, what you're really about.*

Sapphira wavered and worried, but ultimately couldn't bring herself to do it. She couldn't afford to take the chance. She couldn't ask to take him into her confidence when he officially worked for her father. Too much was at stake. There was too much to lose.

Evidently sensing that the moment had passed, Sapphira felt a silent sigh leak out of his chest. "What time are we supposed to be at Ella's for dinner?"

"Six," she said. "We've got about thirty more minutes."

His hum rattled against her ear. "Just enough time then."

She felt a slow smile roll around her lips, then nudged Trixie from Huck's lap and took her place. She smiled down into his woefully familiar face and felt her heart leap into her throat. *Oh, God, she was in trouble.* "Time for what?" she asked, though she already knew the answer.

His eyes curiously intense, filled with revelations she couldn't readily interpret, he leaned forward and whispered a kiss over her lips. "Dessert," he said, coupling the answer with a telling squeeze to her rump that sent her joy juices into overdrive.

"Excellent," Sapphira told him. "It's my favorite."

12

ELLA'S GAZE glittered with knowing humor when they walked into her house at five after six. "Hmmph," she said, darting him a look. "I don't know why, but I'm getting the impression that you take your *body*-guarding duties seriously."

"Ella," Sapphira said, seemingly mortified. "What on earth would possess you to say a thing like that?"

"What would possess me to say a thing like that?" she repeated, her eyes wide. "You mean aside from the fact that your shirt's on wrong side out and his cow is about to escape the barn?"

Impossibly, Huck felt a blush creep up his neck as his hands flew to his zipper. He frowned, gazing at Ella. "My barn door is shut."

Ella smiled wickedly. "But you had to check, didn't you?"

Busted, he merely returned her grin. "I would have checked regardless," he said.

"But would you have looked guilty?"

He chewed the inside of his cheek and took his seat at the table. She had him there, that was for sure. Since lying was out of the question, he merely shrugged and watched Sapphira check the seams of her shirt.

"My shirt's not on inside out, Ella," she said, scowling at the older woman. Her gaze narrowed. "You're sneaky, you know that?"

"What I am, *ma chère,* is perceptive. What?" she asked, quirking an innocent brow. "You think I didn't notice how y'all were looking at each other over here the other night?" She set a bowl of steaming gumbo on the table along with a platter of mouthwatering bread. "I might be old, but I'm not blind." She harrumphed again. "I know what love looks like."

She said it with so much assurance and authority that he almost didn't panic. His gaze swung to Sapphira's and she offered him an equally uneasy grin. He knew he was falling in love with her—knew that he'd wandered onto that slippery slope when he hadn't been able to resist her—but somehow, having someone else recognize what he wasn't quite ready to vocally admit made him feel as if his skin was too tight, his tongue thick, and his body on fire.

On the plus side, Ella seemed to be operating under the assumption that they *both* were in love, and that, he decided, made him feel infinitely better.

Was Sapphira in love with him? Huck wondered. Was it possible to fall in love this fast? Frankly, he had no experience with love. He'd never before in his life cared this much about another person, and didn't know precisely what to look for to know if the sentiment was reciprocated. Odd how that keen sense of intuition he'd claimed to have earlier seemed blind to the most important question he'd ever faced.

Huck studied her covertly from across the table. Watched her small hands—the same ones she'd run over his body, then coated in sanitizer only moments before, he thought, smiling—carefully help Ella load the plates and tend to the table. The two women moved in sync, with familiarity borne out of history, each anticipating the other's move.

While he couldn't claim the history part, he could argue that they did seem to have a certain inherent rhythm. And it was more than the sex, Huck thought, though that was almost so perfect it was as though they'd been making love for years, choreographing their intimacy through repetition and practice. He was in tune with her, for lack of a better description. He always knew where she was, could feel her presence whether she was right beside him or halfway across the room. The idea was as disconcerting as it was comforting.

Furthermore, while she hadn't completely come clean about why she was so afraid of her father and why she'd decided to hide her involvement with Belle Charities from him and the rest of the men at Ranger Security, he had to admit that her trusting him enough to confide in him about her brother's death had claimed another little part of his soul. Naturally, he wanted her to tell him all of her secrets—to share everything with him—but he knew her well enough to know at this point that, if she hadn't, she had a very good reason.

And, dammit, he wanted to know that as well.

Basically, he just wanted all of her. Was that too much to ask?

Sapphira chose that moment to look over at him. Those beautiful green eyes were rife with affection and longing, humor and heat, wit and charm. "You're making me nervous," she said as he continued to stare.

"Good," Huck told her. "Because, princess, you scare the hell out of me."

She stilled, accepting the comment for what it was— a veiled insinuation that he was falling for her, the closest he could comfortably get with a declaration that this was more than just a passing thing. "You're pretty damn frightening, yourself."

Ella chuckled softly. "Do y'all need a moment?" she asked. "Do I need to leave?"

Sapphira rolled her eyes. "What you need to do is sit down," she said. "Everything is on the table."

"Don't get fresh, young lady," Ella admonished. She pulled her apron over her head, hung it on a peg next to the refrigerator and finally took her seat. From the corner of his eye, Huck saw what looked like a moth flutter through the air and land on the floor next to the table leg. Because he was a man and killing bugs was supposed to be his job, he took his napkin and leaned down, prepared to do his duty.

His heart raced and his mouth went dry as his gaze landed not on a moth, but on a single letter cut from a newspaper.

With pinking shears.

He mentally reeled, unable to make what he instinctively knew process. It couldn't be coincidence. *Ella?* Ella had sent the letters? But why? Huck wondered, astounded. What on earth had possessed her to do such a thing? What would make her threaten someone she obviously loved?

He'd wanted answers, hadn't he? Huck thought, sick at his stomach. And he suddenly knew he was about to get them. Dread camping in ever muscle, without saying a word, he carefully picked up the clipping and laid it next to Ella's plate.

The older woman saw the letter, gasped softly, then stilled and slowly turned to look at him.

Sapphira had noticed the exchange and frowned. "What's wrong?" she asked. "Ella, you're pale. Are you feeling all right?" She squinted and he heard her inhale sharply when she saw the single letter. "Where did that come from? Did another letter come today?"

Ella seemed to shrink in her seat. "No, provided the mail doesn't make a mistake, it'll get here tomorrow."

So she'd mailed another one today, Huck thought, still shocked. He couldn't wrap his mind around it. Couldn't make it all add up and resemble anything close to sense.

Another furrow rolled over Sapphira's brow. "Come tomorrow? But how do you know—" She pulled in a startled breath as realization seemed to dawn. "Ella?" she asked, pain, disbelief and betrayal crowding into her voice.

Huck continued to remain quiet and watched the scene unfold surreally before him.

Ella reached across the table and took Sapphira's hand. "Don't be angry at me, *ma chère*. I never expected your father to hire security guards," she said, shooting a look in his direction. "I was hoping to jar some sense back into the man, to make him realize that while he no longer had Nicky, he still had you. I—I wanted him to find out about your charity work, about your mentoring and Carmen, about your time spent in the inner city, because it *isn't* safe and—"

Sapphira gasped. "Ella, how many times do I have to tell you—"

"Let me finish," she insisted. "Please." She let out a little sigh. "I wanted him to find out about how much of yourself you give away, because that's something to be proud of, *ma chère*." Her voice broke and her watery eyes begged for understanding. "I thought if he knew those things about you, he would wake up and let you be who you are—not a pampered heiress but a humanitarian with a huge heart and a capacity for caring for other people that is so honest and true that it makes me so, so very proud of you. You're a good girl, Sapphira, and you deserve better."

She paused and lifted her chin in the same way he'd seen Sapphira do so many times over the past few days. "I could tell a lie and say that I'm sorry, but I'm not. I'd been fully prepared to stop the letters, because I could tell that your father, as usual, had taken the wrong tack." She smiled sadly and lifted a shoulder in a shrug and her gaze slid to Huck. "But then I saw you with him—I saw the way you looked at each other—and if the letters would have stopped coming, then he would have left. And that, of course, wouldn't do." A weary smile shaped her lips. "What was an old former nanny who loves you like her very own supposed to do?"

"Well, for starters—" Sapphira's cell, her ring tone set to Fergie's "Glamourous," suddenly cut her off. She sprang from her chair as if she were on fire and quickly shoved her hand into her purse to retrieve the phone. A quick look at the display made a smile appear on her lips. "Hello. Right. I'm on my way." Her gaze swung to Ella. "I'll deal with you when I get back."

"Where are you going?"

"Carmen's water has broken. I'm going to the hospital." Her gaze tangled with his and she hesitated. "Huck, I—"

"I'll drive," he said, backing away from the table, unsurprised. It didn't take a rocket scientist to figure out that the mysterious Carmen was who she'd been meeting at the doctor's office. Technically, since the source of the letters had been discovered and she was really not in danger, his services were null and void and no longer required. He knew that, but he still had questions he wanted answered.

Furthermore, the end of the case also ended the need to be with her 24/7. The mere idea that he no longer had a reason—aside from being in love with her—to be with her made a needle of panic prick his heart, his palms sweat and a clammy wash spread over his skin.

Sapphira's grateful gaze tangled with his. She knew it, too. Knew that it was put-up or shut-up time and he grimly suspected, after hearing Ella, that the newfound love of his life would opt for shut up.

Why? That was the one mystery he still hadn't solved. But, Huck thought grimly, he was going to. He had too much riding on the outcome to do otherwise.

13

SAPPHIRA HAD EXPECTED Huck to start asking questions the minute they got into the car.

Surprisingly, he didn't.

He just sat there, patiently waiting for her to confide in him, to tell him the reason she'd acted the way she had, to tell him about her father and the strong hold he had over her life and the finances she used to help other people. To tell him about Carmen. And with every mile they got closer to the hospital, with each second that passed between them, she felt more and more guilty for not having the courage to do just that. To level with him, as she knew she should.

She tried to blame her cowardice on Ella's revelation—honestly, if she didn't love the older woman so much and know that she'd had her best interests at heart, she'd be unforgivably angry with her. As it were…how could she be? How could she fault Ella for loving her so much that she'd tried to fix her world the best way she knew how?

Annoying, manipulative and disruptive as it had been, the woman's intentions had been true, and for that, Sapphira couldn't fault her.

Wouldn't.

As for her father, something inside of him had been broken beyond repair when Nicky died and she'd made the choice to endure it when she'd started Belle Charities. She couldn't walk away now. Too many people were depending on her. Did she long for a real relationship? Did she want him to be proud of her? Like Ella?

Certainly.

But she was never going to get that from him because he'd made the decision not to care anymore. He'd perfected the most useful form of self-preservation—a complete and utter disconnect. It hurt. It was disappointing, because she remembered when he'd been a good man, and a part of her clung to that memory, that hope. Prayed for its return, but didn't count on it.

Instead she'd filled her life with things that made her happy, made her feel as if she was making a small but important difference in the world.

In a few minutes she'd arrive at the hospital, would go into a delivery room with Carmen, and because of her—her help, specifically—this baby would have medical care, a home, and his or her mother would have a job and an education.

She *was* making a difference, dammit, and if she had to sacrifice a little of her own happiness—and by default his—then…so be it. She swallowed tightly.

And the time was fast approaching when she would have to tell him that, Sapphira realized.

Huck wheeled the car into the hospital parking lot and her heart ached with the anticipation of the break. He knew it, too, she was sure. Grim-faced, disappointment rolling off him in waves, Huck shifted into park and turned to her. "You can do this alone, you know," he pointed out. "Technically, I don't have to stay with you."

She reached over and cupped the side of his achingly familiar face. "I know you don't have to, but I was hoping you would."

His gray gaze caught and held hers and a deep sigh dredged from his lungs. "Are you ever going to level with me, princess?"

Sapphira swallowed tightly. "When this is done."

Seemingly satisfied, Huck pressed a lingering kiss on the tip of her nose and nodded.

"THAT SOUNDS LIKE a hospital," McCann said. "What are you doing in a hospital? Oh, God. She hasn't hurt you, has she? Shot you? Maimed you? Tried to eat one of your vital organs?"

Huck chuckled at Guy's antics and passed a weary hand over his face. "Yes, we're at a hospital. One of her friends is having a baby and she's the labor coach."

"So you're fine?"

As fine as he could be for a man in love on the brink of being shown the door, he supposed. She hadn't said as much—amazing how what went unspoken could sometimes speak more loudly than anything else—but Huck knew it all the same. The eternal ride in the car on the way over here, when she could have confided everything to him and hadn't, had told him all he needed to know.

So why was he here? Why was he prolonging the

agony? Because he didn't seem to be able to leave. Couldn't quite make the break himself.

Huck massaged the bridge of his nose. "Listen, I'm calling because I've had a break in the case. Ella was sending the letters."

McCann swore. "No shit?"

He felt his lips twitch. "No shit."

"Well, I'll be damned," McCann breathed, seemingly as stunned as Huck had been. "Why?"

Huck relayed everything he'd overheard, every poignant detail, and passed them on to his momentary colleague. At some point—probably in the next day or so—he'd have to confide the affair, but couldn't muster the wherewithal at the moment. Furthermore, that was a conversation he intended to have with all three of them, in person. It was not the sort of fuckup one divulged over the phone. Respect demanded an audience and he wouldn't shy away from owning what had happened between them.

McCann paused. "Why do I feel like there is more to this story?" he asked. "Why would her father give a damn if she mentored unwed mothers or spent her so-called salary on charity work? The man is a total hard-ass, but… It doesn't make any sense."

"I'm going to get those answers before I leave."

"What are you going to do about her father? How do you think he'll react to finding out the letters were from someone within the supposed scope of his control, in his very own camp? I'd hate to see him kick her out, but I wouldn't put it past him."

Because he'd been so wrapped up in Sapphira—in

what the discovery had meant for them—he hadn't considered the ramifications for Ella. Surely Stravos wouldn't kick an old woman to the curb, one who'd cared for his children for years? Huck thought.

Remembering Sapphira's fear, the lengths that she'd gone to keep her father from knowing about her activities, shed a different light on things though. All things considered, he couldn't rule out the possibility that Stravos would put Ella out.

And he damn sure couldn't let that happen.

Huck sighed. "I gotta tell you, McCann, this is looking like a no-win situation."

"I agree." He paused. "I'm thinking our official position needs to be that there is no threat, that she's not in danger, and we're pulling out. That we can't, in good conscience, continue to take his money when we're not making any headway."

Those had been his thoughts exactly. "How do you think the others will feel?"

"The same," he said. "Ranger mentality, remember?"

Huck smiled. He was going to miss that.

"You want to tell me what else is going on?" he asked.

He respected him too much to shoot him a bullshit lie. "Later," Huck said. He looked up and saw a beaming Sapphira coming down the hall toward him. "My target just walked in and she's holding a baby."

"Is there a possibility that she's *carrying* yours?" McCann asked, somehow managing to zero in on what he'd hoped to keep hidden until he could talk to them in person.

She was on the Pill and they'd used protection, but it was still possible. Besides, McCann didn't want the split-haired answer—he wanted the truth. Huck sighed heavily. "Yes," he said.

Rather than the grim silence he'd expected to hear on the other end of the line, McCann whooped and crowed, "Yes! Payne owes me a hundred bucks." But before Huck could make any sense out of what that meant, McCann had disconnected.

Carrying his child? he thought again as Sapphira drew ever closer. A sense of awe spread through him at the possibility, and he felt an answering smile spread over his lips. Unbidden, a vision of her holding a green-eyed chubby-cheeked girl flashed in his mind's eye. She'd have his fearlessness and her mother's heart and, though it was completely irrational, he fell in love on the spot with that fictional baby.

He wanted a child, Huck suddenly realized. *With her.*

"Meet Melina Rhea Martinez," Sapphira whispered proudly. Her gaze slid reverently over the child and her voice was thick with emotion. "Isn't she beautiful?"

"Rhea?" Sapphira's middle name, Huck realized. He'd seen it in the file.

Sapphira beamed at him. "Yep. She's named after her godmother." Her eyes sparkled with unshed tears. "Me."

Huck slid a finger down the infant's pinkened cheek. "How's Carmen?"

"She's doing beautifully. Recuperating at the moment. It went fast for a first baby, probably because she waited until the last possible moment to come to the hospital." Sapphira paused and cleared her throat. "She's asked me to spend the night. Ella's going to bring my bag."

Huck stilled as the implications of that innocent comment surfaced. Here it comes, he thought. She was getting ready to cut him loose. He knew it, could feel it in the very air around him.

"I can take you home to get that, Sapphira," he said, knowing she'd refuse the offer.

She shook her head, continued to hold the baby between them, almost like a shield of some sort. "That won't be necessary. You know I'm not in any danger. You can leave, Huck," she said. A slight crack in her voice betrayed only the slightest hint of emotion. "I've been thinking about that report you've got to give my father and—"

"I'm not going to out Ella," he said. "Or tell him about any of this."

She sagged with relief, the stress leaving her in a wilting sigh. "Thank you. You don't know how much that means."

He felt his lips twist with bitter humor. "You were going to tell me, remember?"

She flushed guiltily and cleared her throat. "I don't know that now is the time—"

"You mean you're planning on seeing me again?" He knew she wasn't, knew the minute he walked down the hall and out of this building that she wouldn't have anything else to do with him. How did he know it? Who knew? Intuition, a sixth sense, a bad vibe? But he could feel her freezing him out, putting up a barrier, pruning him from her life.

And he wasn't leaving here until he knew why.

"Please don't make this any more difficult than it already is."

Huck waited, refusing to let it go.

"Remember when I told you that my father blamed himself for Nicky's death? That he thought he'd pushed him too hard?"

He nodded.

"My father, for all of his distance, is determined not to push me too hard, either. I was all set to go to work for the company, had looked forward to it, and in an instant, that all vanished. Dad killed the job and promptly let everyone else in the greater Atlanta area know that hiring me would make him their enemy. He wields a lot of weight in the business world around here, Huck, and nobody wanted to thwart him." A half smile caught the corner of her mouth. "I thought he'd get past it, that the grief was clouding his judgment and that eventually he'd come around." She paused. "Two years later, he still hadn't and I had to accept the fact that he wasn't going to. So I made a different life. I—"

"Started Belle Charities," he finished for her, "and have been funneling seventy-five percent of your salary into the foundation ever since."

She blinked, stunned, and her mouth rounded in shock. "How did you— When—"

"This morning. Payne did a little poking around for me."

Her gaze softened and a single light brown curl brushed the gentle slope of her cheek. "I wanted to tell you, Huck. I really did. But I couldn't risk you including the information in your report to my father. If he finds out what I've been doing, he'll cut me off." She gestured to the baby. "I couldn't risk her, risk all of them. Mentoring is a personal thing of mine," she said haltingly. Her green eyes tangled with his and the hurt and the pain he saw there made his gut clench with dread. "I was a Carmen once, a long time ago—"

Understanding dawned and he ached with her. "Oh, Sapphira. I—"

"I lost my baby." She smiled sadly. "You and Ella are the only two people on this planet who know that. I'm telling you because I need you to understand why I can't walk away. I can't leave because the moment I do, so does the money, and I've got people who are dependent on it. It's not just me. If he finds out, he'll cut me off. He'll—"

"Sapphira—"

She shook her head. "He'll cut me off," she insisted. "And too many people are dependent on me, including this little girl," she added, gesturing to the child in her arms, "to let that happen. He made himself perfectly clear, Huck. I'm not allowed to work. Period. That's why I'm on salary, to keep me from getting a job. And I can't say to hell with the money without screwing it up for the other people who count on it." Another melancholy smile shaped her lips, and her eyes were filled with hopeless resignation. "I'm trapped, you see? But it's okay, because I'm making a difference. I'm helping people. I'm choosing to do this."

Over you hung unspoken between them and a dry laugh broke up in his throat. "So, let me ask you something, Sapphira. Where does that leave us? Where do I fit in in all of this?"

Her eyes welled with tears. "That's just it," she said. "You don't. He'd never approve."

"Because I'm not rich?" he asked bitterly. "Because I'm a bastard who's never met his father and I don't have a trust fund to keep you in the style to which you're accustomed?" He was unfairly lashing out and he knew it, but he couldn't seem to help himself. He was angry and hurt and wanted her to hurt with him. To be as miserable and as mad as he was at the moment.

"If not that, then he'd find another reason," she said. "And I'm sorry, but I can't give up what I do."

And he couldn't afford to keep financing it if she chose him over her father. He knew it, even on some level above the pain and anger roiling through him at the moment, understood it. She was sacrificing herself and him for the ability to do things for other people— health care, scholarship programs, food and housing. Payne had been thorough in his search. She was doing a lot of good and he couldn't blame her for being proud of that, of not being able to give it up. It was self-sacrificing and principled and…good, dammit.

She was good.

And if he was any sort of gentleman at all, he'd walk

away and not make this any more difficult for her than it already was. After a moment, he cleared his throat. "Ranger Security is ending our service agreement with your father based on the lack of evidence that you are truly in any danger. We can no longer continue to accept payment for a service we don't believe is necessary. If you receive any more letters, then feel free to contact us at once and we'll take the appropriate action. Until then, consider our agreement fulfilled."

A single tear slipped down her cheek and a hiccup of grief caught in her throat. "Thank you," she said brokenly.

Huck bent and kissed away the tear, sipped it up and squelched the burning behind his own eyes. Damn hospital antiseptic, he thought, refusing to label the moisture what it truly was.

"I'm sorry, Huck," she whispered, and the agony and regret in that simple sentence made him want to scream that he could fix this, that he would take care of it for her. Unfortunately, he knew better. He didn't have that sort of money and never would.

"Me, too, princess," he told her, then straightened like the soldier he'd once been and, careful not to limp, walked away.

SAPPHIRA SWALLOWED the sob that rose in her throat as she watched Huck proudly lift his head and walk away. She told herself that this was for the best. That it was the only way it could be. She told herself that eventually the heartache would ease—she'd learned that with Nicky, right?—and that, despite the fact that she didn't seem to be able to put one foot in front of the other at the moment, that she seemed rooted to the spot and cemented with despair, she *would* recover.

She would.

And on some level that might be true, but she'd never be the same. What was left of her heart was putty in Lucas Finn's big warm hands and he'd inadvertently, unwittingly, carted that part of her away with him. She held little Melina close, sniffed her downy head and hoped that passersby mistakenly assumed her tears were of joy rather than sheer, abject pain. She held that little girl tighter and thought about the baby she'd lost and the children she'd more than likely never have, the family she'd never celebrate with, the love she'd never make again with Huck, and told herself that it was for the greater good, that it couldn't be any other way.

She told herself that and prayed like hell that at some point she'd begin to believe it.

A soft hand landed on her shoulder and Sapphira turned to find Ella standing there with her bag. Her face crumpled into a sympathetic frown and that one lone gesture of caring opened the floodgates to her misery more than anything else could.

"Oh, *ma chère*," she tsked. "You've already sent him away, haven't you?"

Sapphira nodded. "There was no other way, Ella."

Ella wrapped her arms around her, snuggling her and the new baby. "There, there," she soothed. "Everythin's gonna be all right."

Sapphira had heard the same sage words from her dear old friend more times than she could even remember…but for the first time she didn't quite believe them.

14

"YOU OWE ME a hundred dollars," Payne said, his gaze inscrutable, as Huck walked into the office the next afternoon.

A prickle of unease slid down his spine. So McCann had told them already. Fabulous, Huck thought, shooting the man a look. McCann didn't appear the least bit abashed. Merely shrugged. In any case, he'd really wanted to tell them himself, but he supposed since he'd leveled with Guy the others realized he wouldn't have lied about or omitted his involvement with Sapphira. Huck pulled a bill from his wallet and handed it to Payne. "So I guess this means I'm fired."

"That depends," Flanagan said, walking into the room, a cup of coffee in hand. "Are you going to make a habit of sleeping with *all* of our female clients?"

Huck rubbed the back of his neck and squashed an embarrassed smile. "No."

"Are you going to make a habit of continuing to sleep with this one?" Payne wanted to know.

"Not according to her," Huck said, aching for the soft slide of her skin beneath his, those quickened breaths and sleepy, wanting green eyes.

Flanagan quirked a brow. "What does that mean?"

"It means she dumped him," McCann supplied helpfully. He plopped down in a nearby chair and looked on expectantly, as though the mess of Huck's life was going to double as his entertainment.

He was having a hard time continuing to like McCann, Huck decided, scowling. "Let's just say I don't possess the necessary funds to keep up her charity work, and her father's a manipulative bastard who has her over a barrel." He shot the three of them a look that he meant to quell any further annihilation of her character or future conversation. "I don't blame her. I'm not angry with her. I want only the best for her."

"What about Trixie?" McCann asked. "Don't tell me you want the best for her, too."

Flanagan's eyes took on a shrewd gleam and he rocked back on his heels. "My God," he breathed. "You're in love with her, aren't you?"

"You think the fool would risk this job for anything less than love?" McCann asked, displaying the first bit of true insight since he'd walked in. "Catch up, Flanagan," he teased. "You're losing your edge."

Payne regarded him with cool blue eyes, probing and assessing. "It's true, then? You're in love with her?"

Huck crossed his arms over his chest and leaned back against the wall. "If love makes you miserably unhappy, altogether wretched and lonely, then—" he blew out a harsh laugh "—yeah, I guess I'm in love with her."

"I see."

Then that made one of them, because he'd lost all perspective.

"What are you going to do about it?" Payne wanted to know.

"Nothing," Huck admitted, helpless and frustrated. Once again a man of action unable to act. "Because there's nothing I *can* do about it. I can't help her. I can't give her what she needs."

Furthermore, he'd tried calling both her home and her cell and she refused to speak with him. He had gotten a call from her father after the report had been delivered and, surprisingly, Stravos had thanked him for his candor and "honest business practices." He'd also gotten a call from Ella, who'd thanked him for not outing her to Stravos. She'd gone on to say that Sapphira was hurting, too, and she'd asked Ella to pass along the request that he not call or come by, that a clean break would be best.

Meaning that he wouldn't be welcome and no doubt she'd left instructions not to let him through the gate.

"Surely you're not going to let a little thing like money stand in your way," Payne said.

Huck snorted. Only Payne, who was as wealthy—if not wealthier—than Sapphira's father, would think money or the lack thereof was a "little thing." He shrugged. "Knowing what she's doing, the good she does for so many people, I can't ask her to give that up for me. I won't be that selfish and eventually she'd hate me for it."

"You don't have to. Payne Industries could use a

woman like Sapphira in charge of charitable contributions. In fact, I'd be willing to increase her salary twenty percent. That ought to cover Ella's housing expenses as well, right?" The first hint of a smile moved over his lips. "We wouldn't want to leave Ella over that barrel, either, would we?"

Huck paused, absolutely blown away. Was he really hearing Payne correctly? Did he really mean to offer Sapphira a job and increase her salary to accommodate Ella as well? Flanagan and McCann were grinning their faces off.

"Look at him," McCann said. "I told you he'd be speechless. Pay up, Jamie."

Grumbling under his breath, Jamie darted a look in Huck's direction. "You've got to quit being so damn predictable," he said, putting a twenty in McCann's outstretched hand.

Huck shook his head, felt the first stirring of hope push through the desperation that had been dogging his every step since last night. He'd been so distraught, he'd actually gone home to see his mother and grandmother. A quick call to his P.I. had confirmed that the man hadn't uncovered a single thing about his father. It was time to take matters into his own hands, to ask the hard questions. Thankfully, the long-time-in-coming conversation with his mother had brought him a unique sense of peace.

His father's name had been Marshall Winston III. He'd been the teenage son of one of the local wealthy families. When his parents had discovered the pregnancy, they'd seen their promising son's life vanish before their eyes and had forbid him from having anything to do with his mother.

"It had hurt," she said. "I won't lie to you. But I wasn't going to insist that he thwart his family and I was too proud to ever ask for any help." She paused. "Just when I had given up, he'd come back to me—back to *us*." She'd smiled then, remembering, but the grin slowly faded. "I was five months along when he died. Killed in a boating accident out on Fawn Lake. You have his eyes." She'd paused and her weary gaze had clouded with memory. "Anyway, after he passed away, I got a letter from his family requesting that I never contact them. It was so sad. You'd have thought that they would have wanted the only part left of their son—*you*—but…that wasn't the case. I'm sorry," she'd said. "Frankly, son, I don't know what's taken you so long to ask. I would have told you at any time, but since you never brought it up…" She shrugged. "I took the easy way out and never did, either. I'm sorry."

She had nothing to be sorry for, Huck had told her, and she damn sure had never taken the easy way out. She was the most kindhearted, hardworking person he'd ever known and he loved her.

Much like Sapphira, he'd realized. Their qualities were remarkably similar.

At the end of that meeting, he'd come home with the answers to his questions and a cookie bouquet the size of an apple basket. Huck grinned.

Remembering Sapphira's cookie fetish, even the bouquet had made him think of her. He'd promised to share it with her after all, hadn't he?

Huck's gaze found Payne's once more. "I don't know what to say," he finally told him.

"Can I make a suggestion?" McCann said, and Huck turned to look at him.

Huck turned. "I think you should say thank-you. Then I think you should go and tell her about it so that you can get her back and you all can live happily ever after. It's, uh… It's what we do around here," he explained, as though Huck was a little slow on the uptake.

"She won't see me," Huck said. "I've tried. And you know the property. There's only one way in and out and every stretch of fence is covered in motion detectors." He shrugged. "Short of dropping onto the—" Huck stilled as the brilliant glimmering of a plan began to take shape.

McCann smiled. "There we go," he said. "Now you're thinking like a Falcon. Think you've got one more jump in you?"

Huck nodded, the first tingling of excitement beginning to infect his blood. And it wasn't from the jump, he realized. It was because he was going to see her again. Because, thanks to Payne, he could fix this. He could make her his.

Huck shot him a grateful look. "I don't know how I'll ever repay you for this."

A full-fledged smile transformed Payne's face. "You can start by not screwing it up. I'll call the airport and have the plane readied."

McCann whooped. "All right! Let's go kiss some ass!"

Flanagan glared at him as though he'd lost his mind.

"Well 'kick some ass' certainly doesn't apply, does it?" he defended. "And if he marries her, we all know he'll be doing more ass kissin' than kickin'."

"True," Jamie said, nodding thoughtfully. He sighed heavily. "But it's worth it."

Huck chuckled, despite himself, and slapped McCann on the shoulder. "You're growing on me, man. You're growing on me."

"That's because he's a parasite," Jamie said. He smiled at Huck. "Congratulations, man. We're happy for you."

Touched, Huck smiled. But they couldn't nearly be as happy for him as he was for himself.

And right now there was a mouthy little rich girl confined in a gilded cage who desperately needed rescuing.

"I THINK YOU'RE A FOOL," Cindy said, seemingly outraged. "You let him go? You let him walk away? For what, Sapphira? Belle Charities?"

"You know better than that, Cindy. We've been over this."

Cindy seemed genuinely baffled. "Let me tell you what I know. I know that with enough hard work we could have drummed up the funds to free you from this posh prison. I know that finding someone you love— who loves you back—is priceless and shouldn't be tossed aside so easily."

How dare she imply it was easy! Sapphira thought, blinking back what felt like the millionth tear. It hadn't been easy, dammit. Watching him walk away—and the rest of her selfish hopes and dreams right along with him—had been the most difficult thing she'd ever had to do. But unlike Cindy, Sapphira was a realist. If it were possible to raise that kind of money…then why hadn't they? Why did they always have their hand out? Why did it feel as if they weren't doing enough?

No, she was wrong, Sapphira thought. She hadn't made the easy choice, but she had made the right one. Until her circumstances changed, she didn't see any way out of her current arrangement with her father.

But she had gone to see him, and she had told him that she was tired of being on salary without a job. Though she knew it could potentially ruin everything, she hadn't been able to sit idly by and do nothing anymore. She'd told him a bit about her charity work and that she planned to do more. Curiously, her father had paused long enough to look at her—truly look at her. He'd blinked, seemingly startled, then had gruffly given his consent. "Do whatever you want to," he'd said. "I just don't want to lose you." It was the closest thing to affection she'd felt from her father in a long time. Pity she'd had to lose Huck to get it.

And God how she missed him. She'd spent last night at the hospital with Carmen, but had planned on staying at home tonight to lick her wounds in private.

Unfortunately, one look at her big lonely bed had quickly changed that plan.

In fact, she could honestly say that she couldn't look anywhere around this house—what used to be her sanctuary—without seeing him. There, slouched in her recliner. Seated at her kitchen table. Curled up on her couch and, heaven help her, sprawled out across her bed. She missed him more than she ever imagined she could long for a person. That wicked smile, those mysterious smoky-gray eyes. His laugh. She blinked back another fresh wash of watery emotion and dabbed at her eyes with the perpetual tissue she'd held in her hand since last night.

How had things gone so very wrong? How had she managed, in less than a week, to put herself in this sort of position? And there went another plane, she thought, cursing the fact that they lived so close to the airport. Now she'd never hear one and not think of Huck, his fearless body sailing through the air and the resulting injury that had ultimately made their paths cross.

Ella knocked on her door. "Sapphira, could you come outside, please?"

"Ella, do I really—"

"Come on, child. Sunshine will do you some good."

Mumbling under her breath, Sapphira reluctantly heaved herself from off the couch, dusting the cookie crumbs and chip flakes—evidence of her food therapy—from her chest in the process.

The only thing the sunshine was going to do was make her puffy eyes ache, Sapphira decided, joining Ella and Cindy out in the front yard.

Ella shielded her eyes from the sun and looked skyward. "Hmm," she said. "Well, would you look at that?"

Sapphira frowned, cupped a hand over her own eyes and glanced up. "Look at—"

Her breath caught in her throat, smothering the last part of that sentence, and she felt her heart skip a beat in her chest. No, she thought, staring at the skydiver headed right for her front yard. It couldn't be— He wouldn't—

But even from this distance she knew it was Huck. She'd know that lean, muscular body anywhere. Furthermore, she could feel him getting closer, coming into her range, so to speak, where she could pick him up on her internal radar.

He'd said he couldn't skydive anymore. He'd told her that his knee wouldn't hold up to the stress of the landing. That's why he'd left the military, had given up his dream.

What the hell was he doing? Sapphira thought as his form drew closer and closer. She could make out his smile, see the absolute euphoria on his face. And, sweet heaven, how dear that was. Her chest grew so tight with emotion she feared it would burst. She hurried forward as he drew closer, started screaming at him before he ever hit the ground.

"Have you lost your mind?" she screeched. "Are you trying to kill yourself? Put yourself in a wheelchair for the rest of your life?"

Huck landed with a gentle, graceful roll at her feet. "That depends. Are you willing to push me around for the rest of my life?"

Seriously, her damn heart was going to explode. He couldn't do this to her. She had to say no. She'd taken a baby step with her father, but she couldn't see him going completely for this.

She dropped to her knees, her gaze tracing the woefully familiar lines of his face, his hopeful expression. "Huck, please don't do this."

He pulled an iced cookie—no doubt one of his mother's—from the front chest pocket of his jumpsuit and handed it to her. The words "Will you marry me?" had been written in pink icing.

She felt it then. Her heart actually came apart. "Huck, I—"

"You don't have to choose, Sapphira," Huck told her. "I'd never ask you to do that." He smiled, reached up and swiped a tear from her cheek. "But you don't have to. Payne wants you to come to work for him, head up his charities. He's going to increase your salary by twenty percent so that you can bring Ella with you."

If she hadn't already been on the ground, she would have surely fallen over. Even now, her legs felt like jelly. "Are you serious?" she breathed.

He nodded. "I love you. I would never ask you to give up being who you are, unless I knew you could still be who you are…with me." His lips curled into an endearingly unsure smile. Her arrogant caveman, laid bare, prone, and at her feet, unsure. She choked on a sob. "Oh, Huck, I—"

He held up a hand and quirked a brow. "I sense some name-calling coming on. You aren't about to call me anything you'll regret, are you?"

Behind them, Cindy and Ella laughed, and at some point all three gentleman from Ranger Security had managed to get onto the property.

Smiling, Sapphira leaned down and pressed a tender kiss against his lips, cupped his beautiful face with her hands. "How does fiancé sound?"

Huck chuckled, his heart in his eyes, and kissed her back. "A damn sight better than 'insufferable, boorish clod,' I can tell you that."

Epilogue

WATCHING HUCK AND SAPPHIRA seal their new status with a kiss, McCann opened his palm and held it up to the other two men standing with him. "Pay up," he said. "I pegged it from the beginning."

Both Payne and Flanagan smacked another couple of C-notes into his hand and shook their heads. "I'd dearly like to know how," Flanagan grumbled. "You'd never even met him."

"I didn't have to. I knew. I knew the minute he walked in the room and laid eyes on her." He rocked back on his heels. "I'm getting pretty damn good at this love thing."

Flanagan snorted. "That or you're just the luckiest bastard I've ever seen."

"Speaking of luck," Payne piped up. "I heard from Garrett today. He's sending another recruit our way."

Guy stilled. "Really? This soon? Who?"

"Mick Chivers. A reputation for being a bit reckless, but a good Ranger. Same unit as Huck."

"Why's he leaving?"

Payne rubbed his jaw. "Now, that's the mystery. There doesn't seem to be a reason."

Guy chuckled softly. "Oh, hell, there's *always* a reason."

Finding it out, that was always the interesting part.

* * * * *

Don't miss the fireworks when new Ranger
Mick Chivers meets his match in The Hell-Raiser,
available September 2009 from
Mills & Boon® Blaze®.

Mallory Hunt's first meeting with Jake Trinity ten years ago ended in a steamy kiss...and changed her life forever. Now Jake's back to settle the score with the woman who has starred in all of his most sizzling dreams...

Turn the page for a sneak preview of

Over the Edge
by Jeanie London,
available from Mills & Boon® Blaze®
in September 2009.

Over the Edge
by
Jeanie London

The kiss—ten years ago

THE WOMAN moved as if she were making love, slim curves gathering and unfolding in a sinuous display as she descended a rope using nothing more than the strength of her upper body to lower her, long sleek legs to anchor her. She wore all black, from the top of her ski-mask-covered head to the tips of her soft-soled boots.

Jake Trinity stopped short in the doorway leading from the offices to the warehouse, the two sides of his brain colliding at the impossibility of the sight. One side absorbed her smooth descent as she shimmied down and dropped to her feet without a sound, her body absorbing the impact with an effortless motion that brought to mind a cat landing on all fours.

This had to be the testosterone-filled half of his brain. The more rational half observed that she'd landed neatly out of reach of the infrared sensor beams zigzagging across the opening of the warehouse doors.

No one should have been in the building.

The night watchman who'd let him in earlier must have gone to sleep on the job because Innovative Engineering had a state-of-the-art security system, barbed-wire fences and steel-reinforced doors and windows to avoid exactly this occurrence.

Jake knew this for certain. For the past two years he'd

been conducting his internship with Innovative, the largest electrical engineering firm on the eastern seaboard. He'd made it his business to learn everything about the company he was establishing a career with while earning his degrees.

He'd only stopped by this late on a Saturday night to retrieve some account data so he could continue work on a project for his newest boss, the company president.

He remembered his father's parting words as he'd left home earlier. *College students should spend their weekends dating, playing golf and watching football games, in that order.*

Had Jake put any stock in his father's opinion, he wouldn't be standing inside a building watching a burglary in progress.

Not that this particular thief would present much of a problem. *She* wouldn't, but Jake didn't believe for one second that this woman was alone. No way.

He stood shadowed in the doorway as she raised her hand to punch numbers onto a keypad, presumably to disable the beam sensor. He searched for any identifying features to report to the police—if he survived the meeting with her accomplices.

Five feet four inches, maybe five-five, most of which comprised long, long legs...

A body that was all slim lines and sleek curves...

Liquid movements that reminded him of...sex.

Something about her, and Jake wasn't sure what, struck him as young. Around his age maybe. Not quite twenty. With effort, he shrugged off the thought as plain stupid. Why would any young woman be breaking into a commercial warehouse that stored millions of dollars of electrical equipment, not to mention a high-security vault that housed several invaluable prototypes?

Jake didn't have a chance to consider the possible answers because the mystery woman suddenly spun and looked directly at him. She could have only sensed his presence. Her back had been to him and he hadn't moved, had barely *breathed*.

The black mask covered her face and neck. He couldn't make out her eyes but got the impression they were light, that she must be Caucasian, although he couldn't see even a sliver of skin to support the impression. Something about her suggested she was as surprised to find him as he'd been to come across her. Something about the way she squared her shoulders and raised her chin…

He stepped into the foyer that connected the offices with the warehouse, expecting her to run. He'd catch her and deal with her accomplices later.

But his mystery woman didn't run. She only lifted a gloved finger to her mouth and gestured him to silence as she approached. She clearly wasn't worried that he'd hurt her, and Jake thought that said a lot about her confidence in her abilities. Though she couldn't know he'd wrestled through high school and still made time for the sport in college, he was a full head taller and outweighed her by at least eighty pounds.

But her hands were free. If she was armed, she hadn't gone for a weapon.

He stopped and waited, the more impulsive side of his brain noticing how she even walked as if she were making love, all toned muscle and sleek grace. There was no panic about her, or violence. He had the feeling she was challenging him. As if she dared him to play a dangerous game.

So what was his next move?

Jake wasn't sure about anything except there were other

burglars around somewhere, and he wanted very much to see what this woman's next move would be.

The eye slits in the ski mask were wider than he'd realized, but she'd blackened the skin below, like a television cat burglar. He could see two pale-green eyes, so clear a green they seemed to laser through the darkness.

She didn't utter a sound, though he half expected her to say something. The occasion seemed to warrant a verbal exchange, but she only assessed him with a challenge in those eyes.

Jake assessed her as carefully, calculated that she stood just out of his reach. A few inches closer and he could've taken her down with a leg drop that she wouldn't have seen coming. He still could, but he'd have to spring on her to cover those extra few inches.

Holding her gaze, he tensed for action....

In one sleek burst of motion, *she* pounced, covering the distance between them while dragging up the edge of her mask. A glimpse of clear ivory skin, a daintily pointed chin and a kissable red mouth stopped him short.

He could see enough of her face to shoot sparks through him even as the rational half of his brain recognized that she hadn't revealed enough for him to identify her to the police.

That was his last thought before she slipped leather-clad fingers around his neck, raised up on tiptoes...

And kissed him.

Her moist mouth slanted across his and parted enough so their breaths literally collided.

Jake gasped, but she only laughed, a sultry sound that gusted against his lips, a sound that annihilated reason beneath a blast of testosterone that made his bones melt and his glasses fog.

He should take her down and restrain her for the police.

But that thought dissolved the instant she swept her warm silk tongue into his mouth, prowling inside boldly, engaging him in a kiss so hot that she shut down the rational half of his brain as if it had never existed.

Her fingers anchored his face close. She thrust her body against his, a sleek motion that caught him in all the right spots…firm breasts against his chest, her stomach cradling a hard-on that shouldn't be happening given their situation. Everything about her was daring him to take what she offered.

Jake practically vibrated with his reaction, a hunger unlike anything he'd ever felt. Instinctively, he lifted his hands, slipped his fingers along the ski mask and forced her to tilt her face back so he could drive his tongue into her mouth.

The hot taste of passion chased away any worries, any reasonable thoughts…including all awareness of the surveillance camera that was angled at them, recording every second of that incredible kiss.

Rich, successful and gorgeous…

These Australian men clearly need wives!

Featuring:

THE WEALTHY AUSTRALIAN'S PROPOSAL
by Margaret Way

THE BILLIONAIRE CLAIMS HIS WIFE
by Amy Andrews

INHERITED BY THE BILLIONAIRE
by Jennie Adams

Available 21st August 2009

2 FREE BOOKS
AND A SURPRISE GIFT

We would like to take this opportunity to thank you for reading this Mills & Boon® book by offering you the chance to take TWO more specially selected titles from the Blaze® series absolutely FREE! We're also making this offer to introduce you to the benefits of the Mills & Boon® Book Club™—

- **FREE home delivery**
- **FREE gifts and competitions**
- **FREE monthly Newsletter**
- **Exclusive Mills & Boon Book Club offers**
- **Books available before they're in the shops**

Accepting these FREE books and gift places you under no obligation to buy, you may cancel at any time, even after receiving your free books. Simply complete your details below and return the entire page to the address below. You don't even need a stamp!

YES Please send me 2 free Blaze books and a surprise gift. I understand that unless you hear from me, I will receive 3 superb new titles every month, including a 2-in-1 title priced at £4.99 and two single titles priced at £3.19 each, postage and packing free. I am under no obligation to purchase any books and may cancel my subscription at any time. The free books and gift will be mine to keep in any case.

Ms/Mrs/Miss/Mr _____ initials _____

Surname _____

address _____

_____

_____ postcode _____

Send this whole page to: Mills & Boon Book Club, Free Book Offer, FREEPOST NAT 10298, Richmond, TW9 1BR.